Range War Hell

For many in the war-torn county of Fort Such memories of the bloody feud between the mighty Doubletree and Rancho Antigua cattle country giants were re-awakened. This had caused many an honest settler to up stakes and move on, to be replaced in turn by those of the new breed.

They called them gunfighters, but most were simply killers, lethal gunmen and drifters who could quickly convert any troubled territory into a graveyard.

Yet the bloodshed and carnage also attracted a lone man with a gun whom Fort Such had all but forgotten over the years. His arrival brought the feud to explosion point.

Range War Hell

Ryan Bodie

A Black Horse Western

ROBERT HALE · LONDON

© Ryan Bodie 2011
First published in Great Britain 2011

ISBN 978-0-7090-9222-3

Robert Hale Limited
Clerkenwell House
Clerkenwell Green
London EC1R 0HT

www.halebooks.com

Typeset by
Derek Doyle & Associates, Shaw Heath
Printed and bound in Great Britain by
CPI Antony Rowe, Chippenham and Eastbourne

CHAPTER 1

BLOOD FEUD

'Señor Curt!'

'What?'

'Someone comes!'

Curt August, top gun and troubleshooter for the mighty Antigua Ranch glanced dubiously at *vaquero* Miguel Monero and cocked his handsome head.

Standing there in the moon-shadow of a cotton-wood on the banks of Whipple Creek which marked the boundary between Rancho Antigua and its enemy, Doubletree Ranch, the gunman-killer could hear nothing above the murmur of the

5

waters and the breathing wind in the trees over-head.

Yet because Monero had the keenest eye and ear on Antigua, August continued to listen. Eventually, he picked up on what Monero had heard almost a full half-minute ahead of him.

Clearly now upon the night breeze came the rumble of hoofs.

A supple figure garbed all in black, his lean features and delicate hands catching the light as he stirred, August checked out his Peacemaker and spoke in a strangely muted voice.

'Everybody in place?'

Monero looked around. At a casual glance the bluffs of Whipple Creek seemed devoid of life apart from himself and August, yet this was any-thing but the case.

Concealed at various points behind shrubs, trees and deadfall logs crouched the Antigua hands. Even in the gloom Monero's hawk eyes could pick them out. Here, the dull sheen of light coming off a gun barrel – there, the silhouette of head and shoulders crouched low.

'All in place, Señor Curt.'

Watching the trail along which the riders must come, August nodded. 'How many do you figure?'

Monero, a rotund young Mexican in floppy sombrero and baggy white breeches, tugged at his black moustache for a moment, listening. Then, '*Mucho!*'

'Many, eh?' drawled August. 'Good. The more scalps the better.'

Monero, who like the rest of the hands treated the lethal August with wary respect, studied the killer now. After several seconds, and unable to contain his curiosity any longer, he posed the question that had been nagging him ever since August had brought them out here to the creek at sunset.

'How did you know that Doubletree would attack us again tonight, Señor Curt? For they have not crossed our borders in many weeks now.'

Curt August merely smiled at that. He was by nature a secretive man, a loner who made no friends and exchanged no confidences. Monero plainly believed he'd used chicanery or black magic to anticipate this nocturnal attack. Well, let him go on thinking it.

What had tipped August off in reality had been something much simpler than black magic or voodoo.

Yesterday in town he'd sighted Juan Mariano, son of the boss of Rancho Antigua, drinking coffee in Fort Such with Libby McQueen, daughter of Ben McQueen, the iron-fisted big boss of Doubletree Ranch.

It figured that if August had sighted them openly then Ben McQueen must also know. It was common knowledge that McQueen had sent Libby away for two years at a private boarding school in Chicago in the hope of breaking up her romance with Juan Mariano.

That romance, strongly opposed by Don Mariano and McQueen alike, had been one of the main causes of the long-time feud between the giant spreads, which had exploded into open warfare several years earlier and before August had signed on for the Antigua.

The feud had quietened considerably over the past few years, but the very moment August had sighted Juan and Libby back in one another's company publicly less than a week following the girl's return from Chicago, the gunfighter tipped that the flames would be fanned anew.

Those hoofbeats drumming ever louder through the deep night now told him he'd guessed right.

The riders were drawing closer.

To listening ears, the very sounds they raised

seemed to carry menace – the sound of danger.

This was a familiar sound to the ears of Curt August and the gunslinger felt the old excitement pulse through his blood as he readied for action. After sending Monero back to his post, he took cover behind a sturdy silver cottonwood and settled down to wait.

He didn't wait long.

The first hint of movement in the willows across the creek saw him stiffen and a minute later the dark mass of the night riders swept into sight.

August smiled.

For once Monero's sharp ears had proved less than reliable. The *vaquero* had reported many riders, but now August counted fewer than a dozen.

Easy pickings.

August gave no warning. Waiting until the leading horseman drew within easy gun range he lifted his Colt and squeezed trigger. Bore flame belched from the muzzle and a Doubletree man went down in a churning heap beneath horses' hoofs as the gun blast ushered in the lethal voices of the others lying in wait.

The night riders reined in with shouts of wild alarm and moments later August heard the harsh voice of the Doubletree ramrod Olan Pike order-ing his men to break up and launch a counter-attack.

Instantly, the Antigua hands had stepped up their rate of fire as the dark riders broke off into pairs and hammered onwards towards the creek.

The Doubletree force welcomed them with hot lead, and from close by August heard one of his *vaqueros* grunt and crash to ground. Moments later a Doubletree horse struck the water at full gallop and went under, flinging its rider high to land with a mighty splash and a spray of river foam.

As half-stunned men waded for the banks August calmly adjusted his sights then squeezed trigger three times and an almost decapitated figure vanished in a hellish spray of crimson.

The Doubletree assault proved short-lived.

They'd been sent in by McQueen on a harassing raid on the Antigua herds only to be taken by sur-prise by the ambushers. Five men died in that first crimson half-minute before the hoarse bellow of Olan Pike was heard, ordering the survivors to fall back.

All but one readily obeyed.

Young Branch Filmore, only recently come to Doubletree, was ambitious to make a name for himself. Ignoring Pike's command he lashed his mount recklessly onwards, crouching low over its neck while punching a fiercely accurate fire towards the big tree where August was forted up.

The youthful waddy's speed and reckless daring almost took August by surprise. Almost. Stepping out boldly from behind an oak to finish this reckless upstart off in jig time he was forced to dive for cover as lead fanned his cheek. Filmore gained the bank and spurred towards the big tree, cut off safely from the fire of the other Antigua ambushers as he was by the timber.

It was then that the lithe, black-clad shape of August suddenly appeared again as if from no place. Sounding as loud and murderous as a Gatling gun, his .44 emptied its chambers in one continuous rolling roar which lasted just a handful of storming seconds but achieved its purpose.

Branch Filmore and his flashy big bay horse were chopped down at full gallop. They went down with a mighty crash almost up against the gun-fighter's tree, the rider hurled from his saddle like a rag doll.

The stuttering gunfire died away as, from across Whipple Creek in the sanctuary of the timber, came Pike's hoarse cry.

'Is that you, August?'

Leaning his back lazily against a protecting oak while refilling his hot piece, August grinned down at Filmore's bullet-chopped body and made no response.

A taut silence. Then, 'I got a message from Mr McQueen, August. He says to tell your greaser boss to keep his spic son away from Libby – or else!'

August chuckled softly to himself. He took out a slim cigar, lighted a vesta, cupped the flame in his hands and then raised it to the tip of the tobacco cylinder. Puffing luxuriously he hunkered down on his boot-heels and smoked until Olan grew weary of shouting and cursing from across the creek and the sound of hoofbeats was eventually heard to start up and go drumming away into the night.

Only then did the gunfighter emerge from cover to take inventory.

Rancho Antigua had lost one man dead, with two others wounded. There were five slain Doubletree riders sprawled in and about shallow Whipple Creek. This tallied up to a smashing victory in August's book as he gathered up the wounded and got them mounted. Slinging the other carcasses carelessly across his horse behind the saddle he began whistling a popular tune which he maintained all the way back to Mariano headquarters.

Killing invariably left Curt August in a relaxed and easy frame of mind, and there was added reason for high spirits tonight. With the feud almost ground to a standstill over recent months the gunfighter had been beginning to feel almost wasted hanging around Rancho Antigua.

Not any longer.

Tonight's murderous gundown would ensure the vendetta between the spreads would erupt into full and savage flower again, maybe to burn even more fiercely than ever before. The killer foresaw a continuance of his comfortable, bloody and highly paid lifestyle on Rancho Antigua for a long time to come.

August's expectations were proved well founded in the weeks following the battle of Whipple Creek. Enraged by the losses sustained by his gun crew, Ben McQueen waited just two days before launching another and far more successful attack on the Antigua Ranch, striking this time through the Eternal Mountains' jagged line of hills which comprised half the border separating the warring spreads.

Antigua suffered damaging losses. But, under August's leadership, it struck back almost immediately, gunning down three enemy cowhands riding the wire on the western border of the Doubletree and making off with another forty head of beef.

By week's end both ranchers were recruiting extra gunhands from Fort Such and the surrounding regions while every newspaper in lower California carried the headlines which first appeared in the *Los Angeles Courier*:

RANGE WAR RAGES ON BORDER
DEATH TOLL MOUNTS!

For many, that chilling announcement reawakened bitter memories of the bad old days of the feud. There were even some in Fort Such who, in anticipation of the carnage coming their way, put their homes up for auction and prepared to move out, pronto.

Yet as some settlers quit still others arrived. Every issue of the *Fort Such Sentinel* ran advertisements for cowboys to hire out to Doubletree and Rancho Antigua these days. These actually drew some genuine cowhands, yet in the main attracted gunmen, drifters, badmen ... all the seedy elements of violence and mischief brought to the surface by this new outbreak of range warfare.

They also attracted a man whom Fort Such had almost forgotten – a man whose arrival was destined to set a match to a feud already at explosion point.

It was hot as Duane Raybold and Earl Parnell rode the river trail from Richfield to Fort Such.

There was crackling heat in the thickets that day – the burnt, resinous smell coming in on the breath of the hot wind that caught their horses' dust, whipped it high and then carried it lazily across the banks of the river fringed with green cattails where the afternoon sunlight dappled through the willows.

By mid-morning the whole region had begun to smoke faintly, and now all of southern California's Pierro County lay shrouded in a blue smoke haze which stretched from rim to rim.

The men rode side by side, Raybold astride his tall, black stallion with its silver-worked harness, Earl Parnell on his big, ugly, dun gelding.

Raybold, the twenty-two-year-old gunslinger, whom some folks were already dubbing 'fastest gun in the West', was decked out in a tailored grey broadcloth suit, polished boots and spotless white linen. By contrast his companion sported a garish checked shirt unbuttoned half-way to the waist to expose a hairy and muscular area of sunbrowned chest and sculptured abdominals.

Though of similar age and common profession – gunfighting – Raybold and Parnell had little in common where appearance was concerned.

Parnell was the bigger of the two, approximating Raybold's six feet in height yet some sixty pounds heavier, a man whose easygoing manner belied his considerable speed and skill with a Colt .45.

By contrast, Raybold was slender with finely sculpted features. He was often mistaken for a young banker or sometimes a dude gambler. Yet a gunfighter he surely was, and a sharp observer might sense this in the arrogant way he sat a saddle and the steady intensity of light-grey eyes.

The riders crested a rise in the trail and Raybold immediately reined in, his partner going on a few yards before following suit.

'What is it?' Parnell's voice was like the man himself, slow and relaxed. Mostly, that was.

'There she is,' said Duane, gesturing.

Squinting, Parnell finally made out the greyish

blob of the town against the hot yellow of the summer plains. He grinned.

'So, that's old Fort Such, huh? Your home town?'

Raybold was a man who rarely smiled and didn't do so now. 'Yeah,' he murmured. 'That's her right enough.'

Hooking a heavy leg over his saddle pommel, Parnell tugged a sack of Bull Durham from the breast pocket of the garish check shirt and began building a smoke with deft fingers.

'Well, now that we're in sight,' he said, 'maybe you'll tell me what the hell we're doing down here?'

Raybold didn't reply straight away. Memories were crowding in on the fast gun as his gaze played over familiar gulches, hills and arroyos. It was seven years since a scrawny orphan kid had ridden a stolen pony out of Pierro County. Seven years, and this was his first return in all that time.

For some reason it seemed one hell of a lot longer since the young man of the gun had galloped away from Fort Such. Just a bitter kid who knew nothing outside of horses and beeves. Since that day he'd worked as cowhand, faro dealer, bounty hunter, lawman, Pinkerton detective. But for the past two years he'd worked almost exclusively as a gun for hire.

He'd never returned home in all that time, yet this untidy spot on the plains had seldom been far from his thoughts.

He wondered if Fort Such would remember him.

'So,' Parnell said again after a silence, 'maybe now you'll tell me what the hell we're doing here?'

Raybold reined in his rambling thoughts. 'Maybe it's just a visit for old time's sake?'

Parnell scowled. It wasn't like Raybold to be evasive or secretive, yet he seemed to be both now. It was two days since they'd come across the newspaper with the report of a flare-up of the range war down here, two days since Raybold had torn up a wealthy gun contract up Las Vegas way to head south. And in all that time not a word as to why he wanted to visit this dreary nowheresville. Parnell wouldn't buy sentiment; Raybold wasn't the sentimental kind.

He tried another tack. 'Will we be here long?'

Raybold's features seemed to change, taking on that cold expression Parnell had come to associate with this place and this journey. He sensed he wasn't going to get an enlightening answer, and he was right.

'That depends on how long it takes,' he was told, then Raybold brought the conversation to an abrupt end by heeling his big black forward.

Parnell scowled and slapped the gelding's flanks then hurried it along to draw abreast of the other eventually, half a mile on. He made to speak but something about the other's expression held him silent. The nearer they'd drawn to this nowhere blob on the desert the deeper were Raybold's silences, which had first begun the day Duane had challenged and gunned down killer Californian Joe Banks in 'Frisco.

Taking a sideways look at his saddle pard, rugged Earl Parnell had an uneasy feeling that the other looked much as he'd done that day he blasted California Joe into Hades – that dread place where all of their gun-fast breed seemed destined to be heading these days.

By eight in the morning the headquarters of Doubletree Ranch were usually all but deserted, with the working cowhands long gone off about their chores out on the range, leaving the headquarters to the house staff, the yardmen and Ben McQueen himself, who didn't get to ride much any more.

19

Yet on that particular morning, eight o'clock had come and gone and there hadn't been one stroke of honest labour done.

Instead, cowboys lazed about in bunches around the bunkhouses or under the trees in the ranch house yard, yarning and occasionally glancing towards the house where McQueen could be seen with the returned riders he'd sent off some place before dawn.

The yard, like everything else about Doubletree, was huge, yet even the men farthest from the house could hear most of what McQueen was saying. The reason for this was that McQueen was shouting. He'd been shouting and cursing for some time and it was beginning to get on everybody's nerves – including Olan Pike's.

The reality of the situation was that the ramrod of Doubletree was sustaining the brunt of McQueen's venom. And standing in the sun by the porch steps of the house, Pike thought sourly on just how unfair McQueen's attitude was.

After all, it was Pike himself who had attempted to dissuade McQueen from dispatching the ten men south to the Eternals that morning to hit the Antigua's winter graze.

Pike had heard that Don Mariano had trebled

the guard down there, and this had turned out to be a fact. As a result the raid which had been led by charge hand, Rusty Wilson, had proved a total failure. They'd been lucky to lose just one rider, with a couple sustaining bullet wounds in the mêlée.

Yet even in the grip of his resentment, Pike, a shambling yet rugged redhead of forty summers, found himself making excuses for his boss. In truth, Pike had been lying about Ben McQueen and his excesses for so long it had become second nature until he was barely aware he was doing it now.

McQueen abruptly switched his attack from Pike to Gun-shy Martin. Gun-shy had been given the task of scouting the Antigua borders the previous day and McQueen wanted to know why the hell the man hadn't spotted their strengthened guard.

'I-I guess they just wasn't showin' themselves, Mr McQueen,' Martin explained lamely if truthfully.

But Ben McQueen wasn't looking for truth; he was searching for an escape from his own guilt.

'Wasn't showin' themselves!' he mimicked. 'I'll wager they wasn't the only ones doin' that, eh? How close did you get to that fence?'

'Close enough, I reckon, boss,' replied Martin, glancing uncomfortably across at Pike.

'Yeah – I'll wager,' McQueen said sarcastically. 'Livin' up to your nick-name, more likely.'

That hurt. Gun-shy Martin had been known by that moniker all his adult life – and he hated it bitterly. Most people guessed it had been hung on him following some act of cowardice, while the truth of it was that the man was simply shy of guns, had never wanted to carry one. Despite this, the waddy was far from being a coward.

Pike reckoned it was time to step in. 'No point in cryin' over spilt milk, Mr McQueen,' he stated. 'So, why don't we just—'

'Watch yourself – hired help,' McQueen retorted. 'I ain't near finished chewin' you losers out yet.'

The boss of Doubletree Ranch looked the part at six feet six in height with the physique to go with it. A hard worker, rugged trader and one hell of a mean hater, McQueen believed in America, private enterprise and the power of the US dollar.

The things he didn't believe in were many, but what he believed in least of all were Mexicans. And this was the fuel behind the fire between Doubletree and Rancho Antigua which had scarred that part of Southern California on and off for years, and now seemed poised to scar it even deeper than ever before.

McQueen was still venting his spleen when Hank Trilby arrived from town. The Doubletree waddy had been laid up in town after getting shot up in the gunfight in the Eternals, but appeared healthy enough now.

'What the blue hell are you doin' here, Trilby?' McQueen yelled as the hand swung to ground. 'You're supposed to be restin', damn you for a fool!'

'Figured you mightn't have heard the latest from town, boss,' Trilby panted. 'I'm talkin' about the news of Duane Raybold arrivin'.'

There was a sudden abrupt silence around the gallery with every man staring at the cowboy. It was McQueen who found his voice first.

'Duane Raybold? He's in Fort Such?'

'Come in yesterday afternoon, boss,' Trilby supplied. 'And that sure enough set the town on its left ear. Never come in alone neither . . . brought another gunslinger with him, damned if he never. You know that pilgrim what's been all over the papers with folks sayin' as he's ridin' with Raybold – Parnell. They're sayin' that—'

'Quit babbling!' McQueen cut in, leathery cheeks hectically flushed. 'What's he doin' in town? Did you find that out?'

'Well, I done tried, boss. But seems like nobody knows the answer to that. I seen him at the Big Wheel late last night. Everybody was suckin' up to him – you know, jokers he went to school with and that breed what always hangs around any big name. I asked Sheriff Parsons if he knew anythin' about his showin' up, but he never did. All he said was that he reckoned it smelled like trouble.'

McQueen curtly beckoned Pike to follow and led the way into his large den where the stuffed heads of grizzlies, buffalo and antelope stared down unblinking from the high dark walls.

'Pour me a double shot,' McQueen growled, slumping untidily behind his desk.

Pike obliged. Then, 'So, what do you figure, Mr McQueen? Think Raybold's hirin' out?'

McQueen lowered half the contents of his glass at one gulp. He belched. 'He's a gun for hire, ain't he?'

'You reckon he might hire out to Antigua?'

McQueen made a short, chopping gesture with his heavy right hand, a frown creasing his brow now. 'I plain don't know. We know Mariano's been scoutin' for new guns, same as us. I didn't calculate he could afford anyone like Raybold, but I could

24

be wrong. . . .'

He scowled at his desktop for a long moment before glancing up sharply.

'But . . . but maybe he ain't hired him, Pike. Maybe Raybold's just drifted in looking to hire out to the highest bidder. If that's the case then we better put in our offer right away.'

Pike, who'd come to work for Doubletree Ranch several years after Duane Raybold had quit the county and so only knew of him by reputation, pondered for several moments before nodding in agreement. But he had a point to make. 'Raybold will cost, Mr McQueen. Seems I recall hearin' recent how he was drawin' two hundred a week up at—'

'The hell with the money!' McQueen chopped in. 'Whatever it is, we can't pay it. But we can't afford for him to start workin' for our enemy neither.'

The rancher took another slug of cheap whiskey and stared reflectively out the window. 'Duane Raybold . . . you know, I'd just about forgotten him. Hell, I figured he'd gone off and forgotten Fort Such forever. . . .'

'His old man used to own that little spread on Whipple Creek, didn't he, Mr McQueen?'

McQueen's big shaggy head bobbed. 'Correct. Charlie Raybold – a bad piece of work if ever there was one. Got hisself killed one night when me and Mariano shot it out at the creek. The boy left right after that and never came back, so far as I know.'

Pike deliberated on this for a long moment. 'Any reason why he wouldn't want to sign on with us, Mr McQueen?'

McQueen glanced up sharply. 'Not that I know of. Why?'

'Well, I'm just calculatin' our chances of gettin' him. Do you recall if he ever had any trouble with the Antigua?'

'None I ever heard of. Hell, Pike, he was only a kid.'

'Uh-huh. In that case it looks like we'll both be on the same footin' biddin' for his services. That's if you're dead sure you want him?'

McQueen got noisily to his feet. 'I don't want him – that's just the point. And the reason I don't is on account I couldn't afford him. This feud is bleedin' me drier than a lime-burner's boot, goddamn. But if that there joker was to sign up with Mariano, why, it could mean the difference between winnin' and losin' for me.'

Pike nodded soberly. 'So, what about the other

one? Parnell.'

McQueen, whose part in the bloody range war ensured that he kept close tabs on the names and reps of guns for hire, spoke authoritatively. 'He's not in Raybold's class, so they say, but he's damn good. Go get 'em both if you can, Pike.'

Breaking off, he bent over and unlocked the drawer to extract a fat wad of notes. He tossed it across and the other snatched it one-handed.

'That's your retainer,' he stated. 'Try and get 'em both as quick and as cheap as you can. But if Antigua's biddin' too, then there's no limit but the sky. *Compre?*'

'Sure, boss,' murmured Pike, and headed for the door.

Within minutes he was on his way to Fort Such.

CHAPTER 2

SEVEN-YEAR HATE

Parnell sat up in bed and winced as Raybold strolled into the room. Clapping an unsteady hand to his forehead he clenched his eyes tight shut.

It didn't help.

He still felt terrible.

He forced his eyes open to see Raybold clean-shaven, immaculately togged out and looking healthy as a stud bull – which only caused him to feel worse.

'What's the time?' he groaned, wincing again as the other opened the doors to the gallery to admit a bright and punishing sunlight.

'It's gone eight. C'mon, let's go chow down.'

Parnell swung feet on to bare boards and groaned again. 'It don't figure,' he complained. 'We drank shot for shot last night. How come you ain't sick too?'

Leaning a shoulder against the doorframe, Raybold plucked a stubby cigar from a shirt pocket.

'It's not the liquor that's making you feel bad,' he stated. 'All that fool dancing you went on with last night. Remember? You were going for hours, mostly with that little Kitty as I recall.'

Parnell suddenly looked brighter. 'Yeah . . . Kitty. By glory, man, she is one pretty filly. Right?'

Raybold shrugged. Their tastes in feminine beauty were pretty diverse. Raybold liked his women quiet and ladylike while Earl preferred the brassy, bouncy breed. Like pretty Kitty Clare.

Bedsprings creaked as Parnell sat down to draw on his big hand-tooled boots. 'Say, Duane, you went to school with Kitty, didn't you?'

'Right.'

'I got a hunch she's a bit sweet on you.'

Raybold snatched up a damp towel and tossed it at the other's head.

'If you can stand talking about women on an

empty belly, then I can't,' he said, heading for the door. 'Come on. If the pancakes at the Hash House are half as good as I recall that's the best reason I've had to chow down this week.'

Jamming on his hat Parnell banged the door shut behind them, winced, then followed the other for the staircase. Half-way down, an ancient roustabout polishing the hand-rail stopped Raybold and insisted on shaking hands and recalling how he'd 'chased him out of his apple yard' a decade before.

This sort of thing was occurring regularly and Raybold was growing accustomed to it by now. Oldsters like the roustabout liked the way he was raising the dust and challenging the big ranchers. But the old guy suddenly turned serious before they could get away.

'You got the big fellas all twitchy right enough, young Raybold, and bless you for it,' he warned. 'But you'd best watch your step if what I hear about what the Combine might be cookin' up for you is to be counted on. . . .'

That was all they heard before they reached ground level and headed for the diner. They'd heard all the warnings and would take their chances.

Then, 'Raybold!'

None knew better than Earl Parnell just how good Duane Raybold had become with a .45. Even so he was astonished at the speed with which Duane filled his hand and whirled about while that shout was still hanging in the air.

Both men straightened slowly as mocking laughter reached them. They looked down a floor to sight Juan Mariano stepping out from behind the cover of the newell post at ground level.

Duane let his Colt slide back into leather and took the steps down to join the son of the richest man in the county.

'Not bad, Raybold, not half bad.' Mariano stood with hands on hips, a stalwart six-footer whose tailored riding rig would cost a working man half a year's wages. He was cocky, confident and an enemy. His wealth made him so. Duane's face was blank as he folded his arms.

'Damn fool thing to do, Mariano. Seems you're older but no smarter.'

The handsome Mexican's smile could vanish in a moment. It did so now.

'I was hoping I'd find out that the stories about your coming back were fantasy, Raybold. Too bad that's not so.'

Raybold sized the man up. The heir apparent to the Rancho Antigua had matured from a skinny Spanish-Mexican kid with the seat out of his breeches into a formidable figure dressed in style and radiating self-assurance.

A man of Raybold's own age, Mariano was as slim as a dagger, an uncommonly handsome fellow with raven-black hair and a graceful and assured style about everything he did.

Forty-dollar boots reflected the light and a low crowned black sombrero hung by its throat strap down his back.

Even so, on this their first meeting in seven years, Raybold was attired in apparel even more expensive than Mariano's, and it showed. Immediately, Mariano was momentarily transported back to Raybold's early days as a bare-foot boy with patches in his pants when he'd stopped dead on the walks of Fort Such to see Mariano ride by on an arrogant stallion and looking proudly down at him with a a smirk.

The silence held as the two matched stares. Raybold appeared controlled yet his fists were clenched. The other's obvious wealth and self-assurance were all products of his upbringing when the Spanish-Mexican settlers of the region had taken over vast tracts of land.

Suddenly Mariano surprised by putting on a broad smile and extending his right hand.

'What are we, Raybold? Children squabbling in the schoolyard? Welcome back, *señor*. My father, the *patrón*, sends his compliments.'

And so they shook, began to relax, started in talking. Only time would tell where this might lead, but a wise onlooker might predict that, considering their past together and the great difference in their status now, plus the simmering troubles besetting the region, their future might seem dangerously uncertain. . . .

'You look well, Duane. Prosperous.'

'As I am,' Raybold replied coolly. 'Not as prosperous as you, Juan, but then, I'm just a working man.'

There was an edge to those words which Juan Mariano chose to ignore.

'I'll be straight with you, Duane,' he said agreeably. 'This is no chance meeting. We heard you had returned to Fort Such and the *patrón* sent me in first thing this morning to see you.'

'Why?'

Marian's manner chilled a little. 'I think you know why. But I'll tell you anyway. We want to know if you're here on business or pleasure?'

'Well, it seems that's what's on everybody's mind,' Earl Parnell said at Raybold's elbow. 'Maybe it's time we all knew the answer.'

'I'm here minding my own business, Juan,' Raybold said evenly. 'You can tell the *patrón* that. And now I've got to be going—'

'Just a minute, Raybold!' Mariano snapped, and there was a hard glitter in his eye now.

'The name's either Duane or Mr Raybold. *Compre?*'

Juan Mariano flushed hotly. The spoiled and arrogant son of the richest man in two hundred miles was unaccustomed to being spoken to this way. Yet he managed to curb his annoyance well enough.

'All right – Duane. I'm sorry. But you looked like moving on before I was through. I have an offer to make.'

Raybold arched an eyebrow. 'You want to hire us?' he guessed.

Mariano moved a step closer and dropped his voice.

'Correct, Duane. Naturally you must know about the war between Rancho Antigua and Doubletree. It's a fight the *patrón* and myself have sworn to win. As far as we know you have no loyalties to the

Doubletree, and we are prepared to pay you whatever you demand.'

Raybold seemed to remain silent for a long time before saying, 'I'll think it over.'

Mariano appeared puzzled. 'But what is there to consider? Surely you can say whether you accept or not?'

'It's not that simple,' Raybold replied. He touched the brim of his low-crowned hat. 'My regards to the *patrón*,' he murmured, and walked away.

'See you, Mariano,' Parnell said, and made to follow. But Mariano detained him.

'*Uno momento*, Señor Parnell. My father also told me to offer you employment. We know your reputation and we need men we can count on.'

'Me and Duane always work together. So, like Duane said, I'll think it over.'

Standing tall and straight with the early breeze fluttering his four-in-hand tie, Raybold waited for Parnell at the far end of the hotel gallery. In silence the two continued on to Hash House. It wasn't until they'd given their orders and had steaming mugs of hot and black sitting before them that Parnell spoke.

'So, what do we do next, Duane?'

Raybold stretched his legs and sampled his coffee. The diffused light from the windows bouncing off his gleaming white shirtfront reflected upwards to highlight the bronzed strength of lean features.

'Why – we wait, Earl . . . that's what we do.'

'For what?'

'You'll see.' And Parnell knew he had to be content with that.'

They were just finishing off the meal when Raybold tapped the table with his fork and angled his head at the windows. '*That's* what we're waiting for.'

Glancing up, Parnell saw a burly red-headed man dismounting before the Hash House. He frowned and said, 'You know him?'

'No. But I know the brand on his mount. That's a Doubletree horse and if I don't miss my guess the rider is looking for us.'

He surely was.

'Mr Raybold,' the stranger smiled affably as he strolled across to their table. 'Olan Pike's the name, straw boss of Doubletree.'

Raybold rose to shake hands and Parnell did likewise. Pike lost no time getting down to cases.

He'd been authorized by Ben McQueen to offer them paying jobs on Doubletree as gun crew.

They heard the man out patiently. When he was through Raybold gave him the same reply he'd given Mariano less than an hour earlier.

They would think it over.

Pike plainly didn't think much of this response, and immediately began to argue. But he broke off abruptly when Earl Parnell kicked his foot under the table and shook his head warningly. Pike shot another glance at Raybold and only then became aware that the gunman's eyes had turned cold and distant.

This look was more than enough to warn Olan Pike that this was no run-of-the-mill guntoter he was dealing with. Rubbing a stubby finger around his shirt collar, he hazarded a grin as he got to his feet.

'OK, Duane,' he said quietly. 'We'll let it go at that. But can I tell the boss you ain't signed up with Antigua?'

'You can tell him I'm thinking over his offer,' Raybold replied with a note of finality.

Pike hesitated, flushed and uncertain. Then picked up his hat, nodded to each in turn and went out.

37

Earl Parnell emitted a short, sharp laugh as he watched the burly ramrod throw a leg across his mount. 'You sure got him guessing now, Duane.'

'And you too, Earl,' Raybold replied soberly, taking out his billfold and extracting a two-dollar bill to drop on the table before scooping up his hat. 'But it's high time you knew what's going on. We'll go get the horses. We're riding out to Whipple Creek.'

The shared border between the 15,000-acre Doubletree Ranch and its 20,000-acre neighbour, Rancho Antigua, was eight miles long. Six and a half of those border miles were shaped by the Eternal Mountains, a steep and lofty range of razorbacks running almost due north and south. The northern tip of the Eternals was the source of Whipple Creek, a tiny stream which wound down out of the mountains then crossed two miles of some of the finest grazing land in the country.

Whipple Creek, as Raybold pointed out when they reached the old homestead, was now the official border between the two giants.

Seven years earlier this border had been impressively wider, as wide in fact as the four-section spread which he and his father had operated together following the death of his mother when he was just eight years of age.

It was understandable for Parnell to ask, 'Which one of them bought your pa out, Duane?'

Raybold, wearing that same expression that Parnell had grown familiar with whenever they touched upon his early life, stood on the decaying gallery of the old frame house idly flicking rose berries in the direction of the disused well standing in the centre of the yard.

'Neither,' he murmured, glancing up at the majestic loft of the Eternals. 'I reckon if you were to look up the records at Fort Such you'd be sure to find that these sections are registered in the name of Charlie Raybold.'

Hunkered down in the shade with an unlighted cigarette dangling from his lips, Parnell wrinkled his brow.

'How come, Duane?'

Raybold sucked in a deep breath and his voice took on a strange quality as if it was bouncing back out of some forgotten corridor of time.

'My old man was always what you might call no-account, Earl. Leastways that's how they thought of him hereabouts. And I suppose they were right enough, at that. He got into a whole bunch of trouble and wasn't too keen on the notion of working. He also liked to liquor up good most Saturday nights.'

Parnell grinned. 'Hell, if you kicked out every pilgrim in the West with those kind of habits there'd be next to nobody left to handle the chores.'

'Yeah, that's pretty much how I see it too. But anyway, like I say, I didn't have any phoney notions about my old man. I knew his good points like I knew his bad. But he was a good pa to me.'

Raybold paused, gazing out over the rolling acres of Doubletree. Then he added, 'And he'd still be here pottering about and getting a skinful Saturday nights, but for them.'

'Doubletree?'

'Both. Doubletree and Rancho Antigua.'

'How come?'

Raybold suddenly quit picking ramblers.

'Like you've likely figured, Earl, this here feud between Doubletree and Rancho Antigua has been either sputtering or flaring for years. Nobody recalls how it began although a lot reckon as how it was simply on account Ben McQueen can't stomach Mexicans.'

'Him and a lot of others around here, I reckon.'

40

'Sure. It stinks, but that's how some folks are. Anyway, trouble was either blowing up or dying down back in those days. It blew up real good one windy night in September and somehow my old man got himself mixed up in it.'

He paused to look Parnell directly in the eye.

'They killed him, Earl. Don't ask me details, like who did it and suchlike. But Pa got tangled up with those mobs when they clashed head on up yonder there by those cottonwoods. I found him next morning, shot to doll-rags.'

'Hell, no wonder you've always been so touchy on the subject, Duane,' Parnell muttered. 'That must have been hell, you being just a shavetail and all.'

'Yeah . . . hell. He was all I had.'

'So, is that why you finally came back? On account of what happened your pa?'

'Correct.'

Another silence. Then, 'Can I take a guess? You're fixing to take over the spread again?'

Raybold shook his head, and when he spoke his voice was low.

'No, that's not it, Earl. I've come back to get square at last.'

Parnell stared at him and knew he was deadly serious.

41

'After all this time, Duane? Seven years?'

'I said I had to wait until I was up to the job. If I'd come back too young they'd have killed me just like they did Pa. They won't kill me now. They're at one another's throats again, and I know how to use that to bring them down. *All* of them!'

By now, Parnell's eyes were stretched wide. 'But how? You fixing to play one off against the other, mebbe?'

'You're sharp, pard. That's how the game will play out. I figured it all out on my way down from Las Vegas. I reckon it's so good it can't fail. You're going to sign up on one side, with me on the other. That way they won't be able to stop the war once it's blazing, you and me will see to that.'

'But . . . on different sides. . . .'

'That's right,' Raybold affirmed, full in the grip of his strange excitement now. 'Can't you see it, Earl? You saw the way they came chasing after us this morning, looking to hire our guns. They're itching to get us on the payroll. Well, we'll see they get what they want. We'll give them so much fighting there won't be anybody left to fight in the end.'

'Hold hard, pard. You realize what you're proposing? We could maybe see half the county wiped out if we—'

42

'So?' Raybold cut in, and his face was hard as flint.

'That was never our way, man. We play the game hard but not that h—'

'Then we'll play it by the rules again. *After* all accounts are settled. Remember what I'm owed?'

More words came to Raybold's lips but died there. *Remember what I'm owed!* Those were words that hit home hard, bringing back memories of the pain and loss – the cold-blooded cruelty he had been unable to prevent as a boy.

But now he was a man.

'New game new rules, pard. We're not fighting for money or glory here. We're fighting for revenge.' Raybold paused, one eyebrow arching. 'Or am I getting ahead of myself? Are you with me or aren't you?'

It was a tough one for Earl Parnell to answer. He knew a man didn't just ride back after seven years and calmly set about filling graves left and right all because of a bad turn of the cards way back in time.

But he couldn't let his pard down. The two went too deep for that, and he didn't need reminding that Raybold had saved his life on at least two occasions in the past. He owed him loyalty if nothing else.

But maybe he should make one last try to talk him around.

'I doubt the plan would work, Duane,' he said casually. 'Good as it is. But think about it. There's no way they'd be prepared to fight to the last man . . . the way you say they would. They couldn't be that mule-stupid. They'd both holler truce long before it went that far.'

'I've already figured on that, and I've worked out what I'll do if and when that happens. Well, I gotta have your answer now, Earl. Are you with me?'

'Hell, Duane, you make it hard on a—'

'Yes or no.'

A long pause, and finally Parnell shrugged and sighed. 'OK, I guess it's got to be yes.'

Raybold's smile flashed. He clapped the other on the shoulder.

'Knew you wouldn't fail me. Well, we'll meet each night at midnight to make our plans for the following day. That way we can go on fighting until they're both whittled down to nothing and we're the big winners. Sound right?'

'Sure . . . I guess. . . .'

'Settled then. I'll sign on with McQueen and you with Mariano. Suit?'

44

What could Parnell say?

'Suits.'

Within the minute a high-spirited Raybold was mounting up to go splashing across Whipple Creek and, with a vigorous wave, dropped from sight – leaving the most sober man in the county sitting his saddle and staring back at the crumbling little house.

He tried to picture what it must have been like seven years earlier . . . Duane a gangling, scared kid crouching in there, listening to the hellish roar of battle, the next day finding his father riddled with lead and nobody giving one sweet damn.

Maybe, just maybe, he mused, if he'd been in Duane's shoes he might be plotting his revenge right now, just as Duane was.

This piece of reasoning helped Earl Parnell feel easier in his mind about what he'd just agreed to as he kicked his horse and headed for Antigua headquarters.

And yet some of the uneasiness clung to him as the animal broke into a canter. He was a man who could at times believe in things like luck and omens – good and bad. It seemed that hour gripped him with a clammy feeling of threatening disaster as he let his mount pick its own way around the foothills of the Eternal Mountains, before cutting directly across the open rangeland for Don Mariano's hacienda.

CHAPTER 3

NEW GUNS IN THE GAME

Raybold had figured it right when he predicted that both Antigua and Doubletree would jump at the chance to sign them on, and the galvanizing news that he had signed on with McQueen, while Parnell had joined up with Mariano, swept through Fort Such and the county like a brush fire in July, leaving excitement, speculation and no small backwash of apprehension in its wake.

What in hell did this unexpected development mean? A stand-off with each strengthened side now reluctant to tackle the other? Or would it bring on the final conflict the county dreaded, leaving chaos and destruction in its wake?

Who could tell?

An answer of a kind came in blood and gunsmoke several nights later when the Antigua men struck the southern perimeter of the Doubletree near the Eternals, ran off thirty beeves and wounded two hands under the combined leadership of Parnell and Curt August.

Rancho Antigua struck again at first light the very next day, stampeding a big beef gather miles deep across Doubletree land, losing one of their number but wounding several riders of the Doubletree.

The days which followed were highly reminiscent of some of the fiercer skirmishes behind the lines in wartime, led by McQueen and supported by new gun, Raybold.

During that week both Raybold and Parnell earned their high fees many times over.

In their saddles day and night, each riding at the head of a squad of cowboys from the two outfits, they rode the wide stretches of their respective ranges, always avoiding meeting one another yet still the target for snipers' guns and survivors of vicious skirmishes.

It was their familiarity with range wars like this, combined with each man's gun talent, that enabled them to come through unscathed while less gifted gunfighters were frequently wounded and occasionally killed.

Raybold quickly became a hero to every rider on Doubletree and he filled that role well with his impressive appearance and manner backed up by an uncanny skill with the guns and further bolstered by his personality and leadership skills.

He gave the enemy hell and led so many successful raids that nobody seemed to have reason to stop and think why it was that the spread's defences, totally in his hands, proved so poor.

Parnell enjoyed a similar status at Rancho Antigua, distinguishing himself in the mêlées and ambushes with his speed and coolness under fire. Just as the Doubletree hands quickly grew to count upon Raybold, so too were the Antigua crew prepared to follow Parnell wherever he might lead. Don Mariano, an aged and impressive aristocrat grown bitter in recent years as he fought his endless battle against the enemy, quickly recognized Parnell's abilities and lost no time elevating him a position of equal authority to August's high status.

In so doing Mariano sowed seeds of future unrest. Vain and dangerous, Curt August had objected to the hiring of Parnell from the outset. Not only did August resent the competition but was driven by a fierce gunfighter's pride and vanity.

So the seeds of future conflict were sown between highly dangerous men while the tempo of the range war stepped up, so much so that no cowhand or *vaquero* from either spread dared travel abroad by night unless heavily supported by men with rifles.

It was the eighth day following the recruitment of Raybold and Parnell that something occurred in the region which had never happened before – when violence exploded in Fort Such itself.

In the past the town had provided an unofficial no-man's land for both factions, where you drank with your own outfit and didn't go out of your way to stir up trouble if your enemies from the opposing spread might show up ready to tie one on you.

But now too many were dying. Men with a thirst for vengeance were confronted on the streets of the town by men who the day previous might have gunned down a friend. Tensions ran high and it plainly wouldn't have taken much to turn the potential fire now simmering into an all-out war which could well envelop the town itself.

Nonetheless, that major clash which often threatened to come, somehow didn't erupt until the night the illicit romance between the youthful heirs to their respective cattle kingdoms, the Doubletree and its rival Rancho Antigua, finally became common knowledge. After that there was no stopping the warring faction.

Raybold's face was momentarily highlighted in crimson in the gloom of the gallery as he drew strongly on his cheroot.

'McQueen wants me to hit the Antigua's marshalling yards at Table Rock graze tomorrow,' he was telling Parnell. 'Wants me to get back those three horses you ran off three nights back.'

Earl Parnell had had a hard day of it. Ten hours in the saddle with the Antigua crew followed by a ride into town to visit Kitty Clare, then back out to Whipple Creek in the dark. Too much in one day.

He yawned and stretched. 'OK, Duane, I'll talk August into taking the boys south tomorrow. Or, leastwise I'll try. Man, that gunslick's getting ornerier every day. Seems everything I say he goes against me.'

'Well, in that case why don't you suggest a

double guard on the marshalling yard?'

Parnell frowned, then grinned. 'Hey, maybe that wouldn't be a bad notion. Anyway, you just leave it to me, pard. I'll make dead sure there's no real force there tomorrow.'

'Y'know, come to think of it,' Raybold said after a pause, 'we might as well make double use of that. I'm suddenly figuring I could pull the guard away from the south section tomorrow. And while you're busy *not* guarding the marshalling yards, why, you could hit the Doubletree stock down south.'

Parnell frowned as he thrust his hat back from glossy black curls, his teeth showing pearly white in the gloom.

'Wouldn't that maybe look a tad obvious, Duane? I mean, every time you hit I'm not there, and vice versa. If we both ain't where we should be on the same day, wouldn't that maybe give us away?'

'They wouldn't wake up if you lit a fire under them – neither one of them,' Raybold cut in harshly. 'And you know why, man? It's on account we're doing their killing for them and they're so damned busy counting the dead on the other side they don't even bother tallying their own.'

Earl Parnell sighed in acknowledgment of the truth of that.

Just yesterday he'd reported the loss of two men in a clash in the Eternals, and Don Mariano replied by asking how he'd fared in the previous night's raid on the Doubletree round-up camp. On learning that Parnell had reported a victory there Mariano had offered his congratulations and hadn't mentioned the dead men from the Eternals again.

Stretching his powerful body and yawning again, Parnell said, 'I'm pretty well beat I don't mind telling you, Duane. If there's nothing else I'll be heading for the blankets.'

'I guess that's all, Earl.'

Parnell started down the steps, then halted. 'Say, just remembered tomorrow's Saturday night. You goin' into town?'

'Could be. Why?'

'I figured we might meet up for a drink or two. Reckon we could use a little something to wipe away some of the bad taste of all this, you reckon?'

'It still bothers you some, does it Earl?' Raybold challenged.

'No, not a bit,' Parnell lied. 'Well, what about it? We could meet up at Kitty's big room above the Big

Wheel. She'll be working, of course.'

'Suits me fine. I'll get there around about eight. But I won't be able to stay on long.'

Parnell grinned slyly. 'Seeing somebody else?'

Raybold ground the butt out under his heel and came down the steps. 'Like who?'

'Like somebody called Gail?'

Raybold's expression grew thoughtful as he moved out into the bright moonlight. Despite the heavy demands placed upon him over the past week he'd still found time for a little social life. On his first night in town he had what he saw as a slice of good fortune when he got to renew acquaintances with an old school friend, Gail James.

Gail ran a dress shop on Frisco Street and was tall, slender and a genuine lady.

In retrospect he realized that if he'd been less preoccupied with the bloody business going on out here he might have recognized the fact that Gail James had never completely left his thoughts in seven long years.

'How did you come to know I was seeing Gail?' he wanted to know.

'Kitty. She knows everything that goes on in Fort Such.'

'Uh-huh. Say . . . don't you seem to be seeing

54

quite a lot of her recent?'

Parnell scratched the back of his neck. 'It's the dangest thing, Duane, but that little blonde has got me thinking about her all the time of a sudden. Hell, if I wasn't too old and ugly to boot, I might think I'd fallen for her.'

Raybold thought about Kitty Clare as he crossed Whipple Creek and headed back for headquarters a short time later.

Both Kitty Clare and Gail James.

He'd never heard Earl carry on like that about any female in the time he'd known him. In truth, the way the other spoke reminded him of how he felt about Gail James.

He puzzled upon the reason for this as he cut his pace to a stroll.

Was it just coincidence that at the end of four footloose years they both should get involved in romance at roughly the same time and place?

Maybe, he mused. But it wasn't a very convincing 'maybe'.

He halted on realizing what the truth of it likely was. And that was Whipple Creek itself – or more correctly, the fact that both he and Earl were aware of the strangely-menacing atmosphere that seemed to hang over all Pierro County like an evil cloud these days.

The close pards had survived many a dangerous day together and neither ever wanted to take the long way around to avoid a fight – or worse.

With his thinking going that far he suddenly found himself facing the truth. He suspected that both he and his pard were doing the same thing in this strange town – stepping careful and reaching out for romance at the same time to keep from brooding on something neither understood yet maybe even feared.

For surely a man shouldn't try to deny that there was an evil atmosphere that seemed to cling to Pierro County like a dark cloud?

He stopped in mid-stride. What sort of gun-shy thinking was that? This was just another town on a rough-and-ready trail. Nothing more and nothing less. Get yourself home and stop giving yourself the jitters, cowboy!

The talking-to he handed himself paid off, and time soon found him astride his mount and heading out . . . whistling between his teeth.

The ride out proved uneventful, as it should do. Skirting Two Mile Mesa he was within fifteen minutes of headquarters when, reining in to fire up a cigar and check the time, he heard hoofbeats.

Kneeing the black into the shadows of a massive oak, he killed the stogie and waited. A short time later he glimpsed the lone rider far out across the moon-silvered open country, apparently making from headquarters in Doubletree for the Eternals.

His frown cut deep. He was familiar with activity on Doubletree by this, particularly of the nocturnal kind, and so was aware that nobody should be simply riding about alone this time of night. The horseman was too far off to identify in the moonlight. He was tempted to touch off a shot to attract his attention, but caution and curiosity stayed his hand. He waited till the rider had a good lead then turned the black and followed.

He was sensing something unusual about this night rider as he trailed him across several miles of rangeland that led into the shadow of the Eternals themselves, yet couldn't figure what this might be.

He continued the tail over several miles but still couldn't put a finger on what it was about this man that made him tag him this way.

Duane expected that the horseman would be halted by the nighthawk he'd posted in the foothills, yet upon cresting a rise after his quarry had been cut off from sight for a brief period, he was astonished to see him riding off unimpeded into the hills. Directly below, he picked out the figure of the nighthawk – who had obviously failed to challenge the rider – nonchalantly sitting his saddle and lighting up a smoke.

The rider, Rusty Wilson, jerked around startled when Raybold came cantering up minutes later.

'Hey! Hi there, Duane. Can't sleep?'

'Who in hell was that you just let go by, Wilson?' Raybold snapped.

Rusty Wilson looked guiltily up at the hills. 'Oh, that? Well, er—'

'Don't hem and haw, man. Who was it?'

Wilson hung his head. 'Well, if you must know, Duane, it was Libby.'

Raybold was astonished. 'Libby? What in hell was she doing out here?'

'Why . . . visitin' with Juan Mariano.'

Raybold's eyes flared.

'Now, afore you go flyin' off at the handle, Duane, mebbe you'd better know just how things really are.'

'Well – how the hell are they?'

'I-I reckon you must know Libby and Mariano are sweethearts?'

He nodded and the man went on.

'Well, they've been meetin' in secret ever since

she got back from Chicago. Hell, me and the boys just never had the heart to give her away. I mean, that sweet gal gets precious little fun out of life – but now those two are real serious about each other. Guess you'd really have to be in love to keep on seein' one another considerin' the risk they're takin'. Wouldn't you agree?'

Raybold didn't respond. Instead he heeled the black into a swift lope and within minutes was climbing into the hills and following the sign. He stashed the animal in deep woods after a quarter-mile then followed the trail afoot at a running pace. He calculated he'd covered the best part of a mile when he picked up the sound of voices from a high ledge above.

He made no sound as he climbed to the higher level where he spied a man and a woman in each other's arms silhouetted against a moonlit sky.

He coughed deliberately.

The couple broke apart and Mariano cursed as Duane flashed his gun.

'Keep your hands where I can see them, Mariano. Libby, what in hell is the meaning of this?'

Libby McQueen, a spirited and pretty brown-haired girl of just twenty was for the moment unable to find her voice. During the week Duane had been on her father's payroll, she'd come to know Raybold as easy-going and gentlemanly, strangely at odds with his reputation. But the Duane Raybold standing here in the night fixing her with an accusing stare seemed like a stranger before she looked appealingly up at Mariano.

'What the hell business is it of yours what we do, Raybold?' the Mexican challenged. 'Your job is killing, not riding herd on women.'

Ignoring the thrust, Raybold said, 'You know how Ben would feel about this, Libby?'

'I no longer care how Pa feels, Duane,' Libby retorted, lifting her chin defiantly. 'The way he and Don Mariano carry on about us is quite ridiculous. They imagine they can stop us seeing one another simply because they yell and shout and threaten to wage war. Well, they can't. I love Juan and he loves me, and we'll continue seeing one another until those two foolish old men realize how stupid they look carrying on – and simply let us go get married!'

'Satisfied now – gunfighter?' Mariano challenged.

Raybold jerked a thumb over his shoulder.

'You get going, Libby. Go back to headquarters

and don't try this caper again, otherwise I'll go to your father.'

Mariano made to object but Raybold silenced him with a word. Angry and uncertain, the girl stood indecisively for a long moment then abruptly turned and kissed Mariano on the cheek.

'I'm sorry, darling. But if I don't do as I'm ordered then Pa will find out and send me away again. I couldn't endure that.'

She turned swiftly to fix Raybold with a challenging look. 'You promise me no harm shall come to Juan, Duane?'

'On your way, Libby,' he replied softly.

'You're a man without any heart, Duane Raybold!' she cried emotionally and suppressing tears, swung astride and rode off down the trail.

'You have a skill for bullying women, gunfighter,' Mariano said coldly.

'That's not all I'm good at,' Raybold countered, right hand still resting on gun butt. 'I know how to carry out orders as well, and I'm ordering you not to see her again. You *compre*?'

Mariano's handsome features paled in the moonlight and dark eyes flared. 'The devil you say! I do not take orders from any gunfighter!'

'You'll either take orders from me or take a

bullet. Take your pick. I don't give much of a damn which.'

Mariano shook his head. 'What is making you sound so crazy, Raybold?'

'Just take my advice and there won't be any more trouble, mister.'

Downtrail, they heard Libby's horse start up then fade away. The Mexican studied Raybold a moment. 'Why did you sign up with Ben McQueen? And what made you choose Doubletree to fight for?'

'You wouldn't even begin to understand.'

'And why not?'

'How could you? You never knew what it was like to be poor. You never—'

He broke off. Mariano drew closer. 'Go on, Duane.'

'Go to hell,' he snapped, angry at revealing something of himself.

But Mariano just shook his head. 'I think I understand. 'You are not fighting for McQueen but against us because you resent our wealth. . . .' He paused, puzzled. 'But McQueen is wealthy also . . . so this does not make sense. . . .'

'Nothing you've said tonight makes sense, mister. Fork leather and keep to your own side of the fence from here on in.'

Mariano made to move away, but something held him and caused him to turn back.

'By the Virgin that is it!' he gasped, snapping his fingers. 'You are fighting for neither ranch, Señor. You fight just so that the fighting will have to continue. You fight because you hate both my father and Ben McQueen and you want to keep on until they bring one another down—'

Raybold whipped out his .45, angered that the man had seen through him so easily.

'I won't tell you again,' he hissed. 'Go ahead – fork leather!'

Mariano merely shrugged. 'Very well, I shall go. You see, it matters to me little why you joined in this war, Raybold. It is all madness, and your madness is no worse than my father's or Ben McQueen's. You three are all of a kind. And that is a strange, sad truth, is it not?'

Raybold stood still and remote upon the rock ledge for a long time after the hoofbeats of Juan Mariano's horse had faded into the mountain stillness.

His face was still pale and taut as he finally housed his .45 and took the trail leading downwards.

He found Libby McQueen waiting where he had cached his mount, and somehow was not surprised.

'You . . . you didn't hurt Juan, did you Duane?' she said anxiously.

'He talks too much, that pilgrim.' Raybold said sharply as they set off for the flats. 'You're aware of that, aren't you?'

'What I know is that when Juan talks he makes a lot of sense. But, is he all right, Duane?'

'For the time being, I guess he is. But if he's got plans go on with these moonlight meetings, he's just as likely to end up getting himself killed. I shouldn't have to tell you that.'

'No, you shouldn't,' the girl agreed gravely. 'I know what you say is so, just as I understand the risk Juan and I take every time we meet. But that won't stop us – nothing can.'

'The hell you say!' Raybold snapped irritably and, upon gaining the flat country, rode on ahead deliberately, wrapped in his own thoughts now, silent and aloof.

Libby McQueen was puzzled to realize that for some strange reason she felt almost sorry for the gunfighter. Despite her youth she was very much a woman, and womanlike she sensed the bitterness in this man – the kind of hurt she believed might only be eased upon a woman's gentle breast. . . .

Yet young and gentle as she was, Libby also understood much about how things worked and how the way life often evolved for men of the gun. No gentle woman could ever tame Duane Raybold, she suspected. She feared that it was possible – probable even – that the only way he might ever get to find peace and escape the dark furies that drove him on would be in the arms of that dark mistress of eternal love – Madame Death.

CHAPTER 4

REMEMBER
THE PAST

Even though the old ways were rapidly changing, Don Luis Mariano still clung fiercely to the customs of the past whenever possible.

One such long-held habit that harkened back to a richer, more gracious and less troublesome era was the formal evening meal that was a feature of his grand household. The don refused to break bread with anything less than the full ceremonial trimmings, which at the Rancho Antigua hacienda meant silent and efficient servants, the soft glint of light upon expensive silver and the very finest of foods. Even at breakfast.

Yet even the don was aware that sunny morning at breakfast with wife and son that no degree of formality or ritual could disguise the harsh reality of the world which lay mere feet away just beyond the three-foot thick walls of the great house.

Don Luis refused to discuss ranch affairs at table, yet there could be no denying that trouble had never thrown so heavy a gloom over all Rancho Antigua as was the case right now.

There was far too much violence and uncertainty had become a constant, unwelcome guest at table of late. Down below in the bunkhouses, five men were laid up from bullet wounds, while upon the big knoll west of the headquarters the presence of fresh graves made grilled ham and fresh-baked delicacies difficult to enjoy.

Yet despite the problems of an ever-worsening range war, these issues were not the main reason for the don's brooding silence during that meal. Yet it was not until his wife, a frail, Spanish gentlewoman of great refinement, though failing visibly in health as the death toll mounted ever higher, had left the room, that the Don chose to reveal the reason for his displeasure to his son.

'You were very late last evening, Juan.'

Juan, solemn-faced and handsome in tight-fitting riding trousers and a full, frilled white shirt, toyed with his untasted breakfast and offered no reply.

'You were not in the town,' accused the don, a small, finely boned aristocrat with a piercing stare and a silver goatee. He dressed in the same formal and expensive fashion as his grandfather and his father before him – that Spanish nobleman who had founded Rancho Antigua fifty years earlier.

'How can you be so sure?' Juan replied, not wishing to be drawn into an argument yet unable to stay out.

'I had Parnell keep an eye open for you.'

Juan lifted his head with resentment glinting in dark eyes. 'This surely is something new is it not, Father? Hiring gunmen to keep check on me?'

'It should not be necessary for me to have anybody supervise you.'

'It is not necessary! I'm a man now, can't you see?'

Don Luis nodded gravely. 'Yes, you are a man, my son. But because you are a man does not mean you are above error.' He paused, searching for the right words. His tone was gentle as he continued. 'Forget her, Juan. It can only cause you grief. It will bring her grief also if the situation continues.'

Juan rose angrily from the table.

'We've had this out before, *Patrón*. And always we go round and round in the same old way and end up snarling at one another. I have told you before and I will say it yet again now. I love this woman with all my heart and I shall never permit anything to stand between us.'

Don Luis stood stiffly, dabbing at dry lips with a fine linen table napkin.

'I cannot understand how you could so much as speak to any girl who is the daughter of a man who makes a public boast of his loathing for all things Spanish and Mexican. Have you no pride? Do you not realize—?'

'The men are growing impatient, Father,' Juan broke in rudely, gazing out into the courtyard.

Anger glinted in Don Luis's eyes for a moment, then was gone. He sighed and crossed to the window, placed a delicate hand on his son's shoulder.

'We have always been close, you and I, my son. I hope the love between us is strong enough to survive even this.'

Touched by the simple words, Juan made as if to speak as Don Luis went out, but changed his mind.

Outside, Don Luis took down a low-crowned,

flat-brimmed black hat from the hat-rack in the hallway. He placed it carefully upon his head then stepped out upon the massive pillared portico of the hacienda.

Grouped about the broad stone steps of the gallery were ranch foreman Juan Palo, Curt August and new hand Earl Parnell. They appeared to be arguing, but broke off at the sound of the don's hard heels upon the marble flagstones.

The trio greeted him with respect, and Don Luis spoke, 'Is this not too fine a morning for bickering, *hombres*?'

Curt August, black-clad from head to toe as customary, and looking every inch the professional killer of men that he was, arched a dark eyebrow at Parnell. 'Maybe it is at that, Don Luis. But Parnell ain't the easiest pilgrim to handle I ever came across.'

Don Luis nodded soberly. The ranchero was a crafty judge of men, and knew what was really bothering his top gun. And it wasn't Parnell's personality. Parnell had come with top qualifications and Don Luis had added him to the gun crew with a salary and rank equal to that of August. The gunfighter resented this and it showed.

'It ain't nothin' much really, Don Luis,' grinned Parnell easily. 'You're fixin' to have some of the boys work at the corrals at Table Rock today, right?' Don Luis nodded and Parnell continued, 'Well, I reckon you need a gun guard, but August figgers otherwise.'

'Table Rock's a full ten miles from the Eternals,' August pointed out. 'And Doubletree's been gettin' mighty sassy since they went and hired Raybold's gun. But I still don't figure they're that sassy.'

'I tend to agree with Curt,' Don Luis stated. 'Do you have anything in mind for the guncrew, Curt?'

'Well, er . . . no, not perzackly—'

'Well, seein' as we're headin' up for Table Rock,' Parnell cut in, 'maybe today would be a good time to lift ourselves a few prime beeves?'

'Perhaps so,' Don Luis said, a taut, chill expression crossing his face. He turned to face the towering Eternals beyond which lay the domain of his bitter enemy. But after a long moment, he shook his head. 'But we have suffered heavy losses while McQueen has been strengthening his line riders. . . .'

'Not down south he ain't, *Patrón,*' Parnell cut in. 'Matter of fact I took me a ride down along the Eternals just yesterday. He's mighty light on guards down there on that south graze – I think they call it Willow Flats, don't they?'

'That is so,' said Don Luis. 'Well, Curt?'

Curt August shrugged. He had no inclination to go along with Parnell on anything, yet couldn't afford to carry his mistrust of the man to extremes. If Doubletree was light on riders in the Willow Flats region then they deserved to be hit. The war was heating up to such an extent now that neither side could afford to overlook any advantage.

'Suits me,' he grunted. 'That be all, boss?'

Don Luis just nodded and the three walked across the broad, tree-dotted yard to the corral where the hands were awaiting orders. While Palo spoke to the labourers, August and Parnell issued the gun crew their instructions before heading for the horses. As they mounted Parnell chanced to glance at August and caught a strangely calculating look in the gunslinger's eye.

'Somethin' botherin' you, August?'

'Could be. Y'know, there's somethin' about you,' August said distantly. 'Somethin' that just don't click right, Parnell.'

'Drat – I won't be able to sleep tonight,' Parnell grinned ironically, patting his horse's silken neck.

August ignored the sarcasm. 'Somethin' about you and Raybold,' he went on, still with that

72

probing stare. 'Seems mighty odd to me that you two should split up so sudden like and then line up ridin' on opposite sides of the fence.'

'I wouldn't fret too much on that if I was you, August. Things could be a country mile worse. Why, you and I might have landed on opposite sides of the fence to one another. That'd just about guarantee you not gettin' to make old bones, wouldn't it?'

August paled, a fierce light glinting in his eyes. But Parnell was already on his way, riding off and whistling softly. The remaining gunslingers seemed to overlook who was really boss as they followed.

August stood glaring after the receding riders for a long moment, then finally kicked his horse to trail them out. He was unaware of Don Luis waving a gloved hand in farewell from the gallery. Luis's son emerged from the doorway just in time to see August loping off in the wake of the bunch.

'What is wrong with August today, Father?'

Don Luis shrugged. 'Who knows? Perhaps it is simply because he does not care for Parnell.'

'Well, I can understand that.'

The ranchero studied his son. 'You do not care for that gringo, then?'

73

'I don't like any of that bunch, Father – Parnell, August, Raybold – none of them.'

He broke off and thrust hands deep into the pockets of his tailored pants and leaned against a column overlooking the rolling green acres sweeping away from the ranch house on all sides.

'Do you ever think back to the way it once was, *Patrón*?' he asked reflectively. 'I mean . . . before all the troubles began? It seems to me that Rancho Antigua was such a peaceful, tranquil place in those days.'

The shadow of sadness crossed Don Luis's features. Yes, he remembered. For him, things had not begun to sour when the feud with Doubletree erupted, but rather had altered forever that day long before when the very first gringo had arrived to throw up his shack and immediately set about shouldering the Mexicans out.

The Americans had succeeded in doing just that in most cases. But not all. While ever Don Luis Mariano had breath in his body and the strength in his arms to fight, Rancho Antigua would stand as a bastion against Yankee encroachment. He would remain a visible reminder to all brash newcomers of an older, better and more durable way of life.

74

'I believe I shall ride out with the men to Table Rock,' he murmured, going down the steps.

'Why, Father?'

Don Luis paused. 'Parnell senses there may be trouble out there today. I have come to respect his judgment.'

'Do you want me to ride with you?'

'You know your mother does not wish you to be exposed to any danger. Instead, you may assist the men breaking the horses for the corrals.'

Juan watched his father's small, erect figure affectionately as he headed for the stables. When the don rode out minutes later, Juan found himself wishing for his father's sake – not simply his own and Libby's – that there would soon be an end to the bloodshed. That Rancho Antigua might once more become a haven of peace.

CHAPTER 5

BURY YOUR DEAD

Doubletree cowboy Carl Varger had a crooked nose, a mean and narrow disposition – and a deep aversion for working weekends.

'It jest ain't natcheral,' this ill-favoured waddy complained to Sime Garrett who'd been assigned to riding guard with him on the fifty-head bunch of primes on Willow Flats that Saturday morning. 'Always seems to me a man ought rightly to be in town fillin' his belly with good liquor and eyein' off the gals at the Big Wheel, or mabbe over at—'

'Let's be honest,' cut in Garrett, a thick-shouldered waddy with a badly-broken nose spread half-way across his ugly pan. 'You don't care for workin' any day.'

The fact that this was true didn't improve Varger's mood any. He was about to retort when he picked up a sound – an ominous-seeming sound. Garrett heard it also. Both men hipped around in their saddles to gaze in the direction of the Eternal foothills. A thin column of dust was rising from an arroyo some two hundred yards distant and they picked up the drum of galloping hoofs.

'Antigua?' Varger breathed, drawing rifle from saddle scabbard.

'Could be.' Garrett sounded tense as he swung up his weapon. 'Damn! I said we needed men out here today. But Raybold claimed two of us was enough for the job, and like always the boss heeded him.'

The pair sat their saddles in tense uncertainty for a further handful of seconds. And then, bursting from the mouth of the arroyo came a solid, surging wedge of horsemen led by the man every Doubletree rider feared most . . . dark-garbed Curt August.

'I'm gettin' the hell and gone outta here!' yelped Varger. 'Looks like damn nigh a dozen of 'em!'

'You yellow hound-dog,' Garrett snarled. And then, throwing up his Colt .45, drilled a shot at the swiftly approaching horsemen.

A rider in the Antigua pack went down fast and a crashing volley of gunfire retaliated.

Garrett died in the saddle, shot through and through. Curt August roared an order and the riders swung off towards the herd. With lips skinned back from his teeth in a savage snarl, August leaned low over the neck of his superb blood horse and drummed away after the fleeing Varger, shouting, shooting and cursing. He drew quickly within six-gun range thanks to the speed of that matchless mount. Aware of danger overtaking him, an ashen-faced Varger hipped around in the saddle to blast off a shot that missed August by a full wagon-length. But August didn't miss in reply. The Colt bucked back against his thumb as he triggered and Varger threw up both hands and swayed drunkenly in the saddle for a headlong fifty feet before pitching lifeless into the long grass.

August instantly reined in to blow smoke from gun barrel, and smiled. He fingered in a fresh shell then turned to ride leisurely away. By the time he reached Willow Flats his gun crew had herded the first primes through the fence and were now hazing them east.

The killer was still grinning as he caught up with Parnell at drag.

'That's what I call easy pickin's, Parnell.'

Parnell made no response. His jaw was set like a rock, eyes drilling straight ahead.

'Somethin' wrong, Parnell? Or could it be you just don't have the belly for this style of work?'

'Go to hell!' came the snarled response, and Parnell spurred away ahead.

It was some time later before he reined in to glance back-trail.

He shook his head. Maybe August was right, he mused. Gunfighting was his natural trade and he believed in it. But this was something else again. He would never have taken on dirty work like this if it wasn't for Duane – that was for certain-sure.

Riding slowly in the wake of the stolen herd now he grew conscious of a cold leaden weight which seemed to weigh down upon his very soul.

Maybe he could understand Duane wanting to square accounts with the cattle barons. Yet the way he figured, the man was going the wrong way about it. That was when he decided to attempt to get Duane to see things his way when he saw him later that night.

*

'*Patrón*! Look!'

Standing in the shade of an elm watching the men at work in the horse corrals, Don Luis glanced up at the *vaquero*'s hoarse shout and gasped. Emerging from the timber flanking the base of Table Rock, was a squad of horsemen. Doubletree horsemen!

The man blinked, looked again, unable to believe the testimony of his own eyes. For Table Rock was at the very heart of the Antigua. How would they dare. . . ?

Those working at the corrals were largely Mexican hands, simple, hard-working men who knew nothing of guns or fighting.

At first glimpse of the oncoming horsemen, they dropped their tools to a man and went rushing for the safety of the adobe work shed.

Knowing it was useless to attempt to rally them, Don Luis stood watching in impotent rage as the Doubletree riders, ignoring the workmen, headed instead directly for the vast sprawl of the horse corrals which Antigua had been working on for several weeks.

The horsemen were led by a tall and slimly built

young man dressed in immaculate broadcloth and crisp white linen. And even before he heard one of his sharp-eyed riders croak, 'Raybold!' the ranchero had guessed at the rider's identity.

The leader bawled an order and the Doubletree riders grabbed up their lariats. Swinging them hissingly above their heads as they galloped in, they began fanning wide on approaching the corrals. Then, with each rider selecting his own sturdy upright, he looped his rope around a post, twisted his end around a pommel and simply kept riding on.

Moments later, ropes snapped taut and horses' hoofs ripped up the gravel as their riders reined them back hard. The big corner posts fought the tremendous pull of the ropes for just a few moments before they came ripping out of the soil, bringing a forty-feet length of fence crashing down in a huge billow of dust.

In businesslike style, the cowboys began loosing their lariats while glancing around before moving on to the next section to be demolished.

Don Luis was quick to come jolting out of his shock. Dashing to his mount, he ripped the rifle from the scabbard, jacked a shell into the barrel and, swinging about, triggered at the hell-raising horsemen.

A Doubletree rider howled in pain and seized his shoulder. Duane Raybold hipped around in his saddle and the six-shooter in his fist went off with a bellowing roar. Don Luis crashed on to his back, his rifle going off again, chopping a branch from a tree overhead.

That was the only pathetic resistance.

Staring out fearfully from the windows of the workshop, the Mexicans watched helplessly as the Doubletree riders completed their destructive assault. Finally, with a chorus of Indian whoops and rebel yells, they coiled their ropes up and galloped off the way they had come, leaving the honest work of long weeks lying in ruins upon the earth.

The whole thing had taken less than a minute. It was a further minute before trembling workmen dared emerge from the building and hurry across to where the don lay as he'd fallen.

There was blood on his shirtfront and the old man looked grey as death. As gently as possible, the workers hefted him into a buckboard and, mounting up, sped back to the headquarters.

It turned out that Don Luis's wound was less serious than at first feared. Dexterous Miguel Monero dug a .44 slug from the underside of his left arm, and a short time later the Don had regained consciousness.

By then August, Parnell and the guncrew had returned from their raid on the Doubletree. Their mood was fierce following the unprecedented attack, and August demanded permission to mount a massive reprisal raid against McQueen.

But Mariano would have none of this, insisting that such a reaction would almost certainly be just what Doubletree anticipated, and so they would constantly be fully alert and ready to fight. He insisted they would simply bide their time and wait for the right moment to even the score.

August didn't like it but was forced to accept.

The same did not apply to Juan Mariano. Up until that moment when the men had brought his father in, bloody and unconscious in the buckboard, Juan had managed to keep himself remote from the conflict which was now convulsing all Pierro County.

Not any longer. Seeing his father's plight, the full horror of the war struck the boy, and in its wake came the savage kick of anger.

This was directed at the man whose coming had signalled the transition of the Rancho Antigua-Doubletree feud from a mere series of skirmishes to full-scale war – the man who'd cut his father down.

This was an insult and atrocity which no proud Mariano could stomach. It would not go unanswered.

CHAPTER 6

GUNSLINGER'S CODE

'Death, my dear friends,' intoned Fort Such's full-time drunk and part-time philosopher and poet Mick Clayton to his attentive audience at the Big Wheel, 'is a cessation of the senses, the treachery of the passions, the errors of the mind and the slavery of the body.'

With that off his chest the orator fell flat on his back, if not actually dead himself then very much dead to the world.

Mick's stylish performance drew an appreciative

round of derisive applause and rough laughter from the Big Wheel's patrons, yet Sheriff Matt Parsons was in no way amused. To Fort Such's leathery old lawman, Clayton's drunken rhetoric only too well reflected the current climate of Pierro County – a grim climate of violence and sudden death.

With two youths recently killed out at Doubletree, then old Don Luis gunned down at Table Rock, death was nothing to joke about this Saturday night.

Finishing off his beer in gloomy isolation, Parsons quit the massive high-ceilinged bar room of the Big Wheel and made his slow way down Frisco Street towards the jailhouse.

Fort Such was a big bustling town which reflected the county's prosperity.

Frisco Street was one of the widest streets in southern California, being one hundred feet across – one hundred feet of ankle-deep mud in winter and knee-deep in dust in the brutal summers.

Being Saturday night the street was thronged with paynight cowhands, brightly-garbed, laughing girls going by in twos and threes and mountain men and gamblers with lethal sneak guns concealed behind silken vests.

Frisco Street was also one of the wildest thoroughfares any place in California. There were lithe and cold-eyed gunfighters in town to wash some of the blood away with whiskey.

'Like a god-damned carnival!' Parsons said sourly. 'Who cares about dead men so long as there be whiskey and good times?'

Matt Parsons took the problems plaguing the county seriously. A dour, long-serving peace officer who was old-fashioned enough to believe that law and order were there to be upheld and honoured, he'd recently watched the feud worsen between the giant ranches with a mixture of disgust and helplessness.

More than once he'd attempted to get McQueen and Mariano to come together and settle their differences across a table, but hadn't attempted that ploy in recent months. Their pride and arrogance, so it seemed, made all hopes of a peaceful and sensible solution impossible.

He'd passed by Gail James's dress shop before realizing the lights were still on. Halting, he turned and looked back at the brightly painted little building squeezed in between a hotel and a hardway store, then slowly went towards it.

He found Gail, a slender, dark-haired girl of twenty, at work in the stock room in back, hanging dresses. As always, she welcomed him with a bright smile and nod. Gail was definitely one of the few genuinely nice things about Fort Such.

Removing his hat and accepting her invitation to take a chair, Parsons made small talk for a spell while watching the girl continue with her chore. Then he bit the bullet and came to the reason behind his visit.

'They tell me Duane Raybold was in here last night, Gail?'

Gail's slender hands paused for a moment, then went on working.

'Why, yes, as a matter of fact he was, Sheriff.'

Parsons chewed his moustache, looked at the ceiling, spoke abruptly. 'Are you seein' him tonight?'

She smiled. 'Now, now, Sheriff,' she chided. 'You are not trying to marry me off again, are you?'

No – Parsons wasn't doing that. Nor was he simply making idle conversation, even though it might seem that way.

'You went to school with Raybold, so I understand, Gail?'

'Yes. Duane and I were always good friends.'

A pause, then, 'What's he up to?'

The girl stopped working. She gazed levelly at Parsons now. 'I'm not sure what you mean, Sheriff.'

Parsons made a vague gesture. 'That signin' on with Ben McQueen, Gail. What'd he have to go do that for? It ain't as if McQueen needs any encouragement.'

'Duane is a professional gunfighter.'

'Yeah, I read the papers too. But why in hell did he have to come back here after seven years and start in stirrin' things up again?'

'Why, I thought they were already stirred up before he came, Sheriff.'

'You know what I mean.'

'Well, I do know Don Luis has Curt August on his payroll now. You can hardly blame Ben McQueen for—'

'I'm not blamin' Ben. He's a mule-headed old skinflint and he won't ever be anythin' else. But Raybold and that pard of his, Parnell . . . you heard what happened today?'

'Yes, I did.'

'You don't sound as if it bothers you much.'

Gail sighed. 'Sheriff, I stopped being bothered a long time ago about the war. I don't understand it and doubt anybody else does either.'

'So . . . it don't bother you none that Raybold's fixin' to make it a hundred times worse than it was before?'

'Sheriff, you're in a strange mood tonight. I'm not sure what you're trying to say.'

Parsons sighed wearily. He wasn't even sure himself. All he knew was that he was trying as hard as he knew how to come up with answers to questions that wouldn't let him rest. He told this to the girl, who shook her head wearily.

'I'm afraid you'll just have to ask Duane what you want to know, Sheriff. As I said, I don't—'

'Yeah, I know – you don't understand,' Parsons cut in, rising. But then he grinned. 'Sorry to bother you about this, Gail. Maybe I'm just gettin' too old for this here job.'

She smiled to show she forgave him and invited him to stay for coffee.

Parsons declined and went back out on to the street again. First he stopped by at the jailhouse, then went along to the Hash House and hunted up some supper. That out of the way, he set off searching for Duane Raybold.

He found him a half-hour later, drinking at the Big Wheel with a bunch of Doubletree riders.

Raybold had known Parsons back in the old days and seemed glad to see him. He bought the man a shot and they adjourned to a quiet table in the corner.

It wasn't long before Parsons got around to asking the gunfighter the same sort of questions he'd been putting to Gail James.

Raybold answered perfunctorily enough until Parsons came right out with it and wanted to know why he'd come back to town. The gunfighter, whom the lawman noted was merely toying with his glass of whiskey, essayed a smile.

'Why do you figure I came back, Sheriff?' he countered.

He was sporting a dark blue suit, white shirt and string tie fastened at the throat with a glittering silver medallion. The lean face was smoothly shaven, thick hair brushed back immaculately from a high forehead. And despite the sober tone of the conversation, Parsons was aware the gun-fighter appeared to be the focal point of attention for just about every female in the room.

'That's what I'm askin' you, Duane,' the lawman replied gruffly. 'Also on account we knew and trusted one another in the old days, I'm expectin' you to give me a straight answer.'

There was just the hint of a cooling chill in Raybold's intense grey stare at that point. And he was no longer smiling.

'That's so . . . we did know one another back in the old days, didn't we, Sheriff?'

The gunfighter thrust his shot aside and leant forward. 'All right, I'll answer you straight and plain. I came back because of the war. I make my living from the sort of troubles you've got running wild on the streets here.'

'But why here – in particular? Maybe I understand that fellers like yourself do jobs that need to be done, even if it ain't strictly within the law. But I can't believe there ain't plenty gun work available for you without you settlin' on my town.'

'I go where I'm asked to go.'

Parsons slowly shook his head. 'No, you weren't *asked* to come here, Duane. At least not by Ben McQueen. You see, I was yarnin' with him just the other day and I asked him point blank if he'd sent for you.' A pause, then, 'He said no.'

A chill crossed Raybold's face at that and Parsons sensed the man's withdrawal as he leaned back in his chair.

'I reckon I'm about weary of this here confab, Sheriff.'

But Parsons paid no heed. He felt he might just be getting to the nugget of things.

'I want to know why you came back, Duane. Just like I want to know why both you and Parnell elected to visit Pierro County at the same time just to make things a damned sight worse than they were before.'

'I gave my reasons,' Raybold said coldly, picking up his hat. 'And now—'

Parsons clapped a hand on his shoulder as he made to rise. 'Just one more minute. I didn't get you over here to wrangle but to ask a favour.'

'What?'

'Quit!'

Surprise showed in the gunfighter's hawk face. 'Quit? You mean – pull out?'

'Perzackly. Look, things have been mighty bad here, but I reckon I had them startin' to settle down some just when you showed. The death rate's doubled since you rode in but I always figured you as a reasonable kind of feller underneath, not the kind that'd want to be responsible for a county fallin' into ruin – which is what'll happen if you stay on. So what do you say? Will you clear off – for old time's sake?'

His response was a frozen smile.

'Why, this is mighty touching, lawman – you all in a twitch over *poor* Ben McQueen and *unlucky* old Don Luis. And now all those young cowboys getting laid to rest of a sudden.'

There was a weighty pause, then an added lash to Raybold's tongue as he continued.

'But isn't this all something new for you, lawman? As I recall you didn't always get to worry so about folks. There were times in the old days, surely, when an innocent man could get gunned down like a street dog here and Sheriff Matt Parsons wouldn't lift a finger and he claimed it was just the luck of the game.'

It took Parsons half a minute to catch on. Searching Raybold's taut face, he cleared his throat and said quietly, 'You're talkin' about your pa now, ain't you, Duane?'

'Why . . . maybe I am at that, Sheriff. Maybe I just can't forget the day I rode into town to your office and begged you to do something about Doubletree and Antigua after they killed my father.'

Parsons appeared to buckle before the other's searing accusation. 'I-I'd sooner not talk about your pa, Duane. That ain't gonna do neither of us one lick of good.'

'You can bet money on that,' Raybold retorted,

94

rising to his full height and upsetting his chair with a clatter. 'And you can say the same about your concern for Doubletree and Antigua. That war will play itself out one way or another – and I mean to see it through. Savvy?'

Parsons sighed heavily as he watched the tall figure stride away. He'd never expected this. Sure, he recalled the fifteen-year-old Raybold's grief and anger at the time of his father's death. But hell, that was seven years ago! To hear the man carry on you'd reckon it all took place yesterday.

Seated alone, Parsons brooded for a spell until distracted by the arrival of Earl Parnell.

Parnell, tall and barrel-chested with his flamboyant manners and a head of black curly hair shining beneath the lights, came tramping in noisily with a bunch of men off Antigua to take a place at the long bar a respectable distance from the Doubletree crew.

The Big Wheel Saloon was, by unwritten agreement, regarded as neutral ground here in trouble-prone Fort Such.

Naturally, the arrival of Antigua triggered off some muttering and cussing initially, but afterwards the opposing factions just ignored one another and got on with their drinking.

Kitty Clare, the Big Wheel's bounciest, prettiest

and most talented dancing girl, wisely chose that moment to put in an appearance by hip-swinging down the staircase to join Earl Parnell's party and professionally distract the big man from potential disturbance.

Earl was holding a glass of whiskey in one hand, the other around Kitty's slender waist when Parsons approached.

'A word in private with you, Earl?'

Earl grinned amiably as he looked at the star. 'Sheriff Parsons?'

'That's right. Will you excuse us, Kitty?'

'Why, certainly, Sheriff,' the girl smiled, and Parsons was surprised to see the tender expression in her eyes as she gazed up at the gunfighter. 'But please don't keep him too long, will you?'

Parsons promised he wouldn't. But he didn't realize his conversation with Earl would be as brief as it turned out to be. For when he pressed the man for the real reason behind his and Raybold's entry into the Pierro County arena, Earl merely shrugged, informed him it was none of his business, and returned to the bar.

It was a heavy-footed Matt Parsons who quit the Big Wheel some time later to trudge off for his office.

The lawman hadn't really expected to be able to talk the troublemakers into saddling up and heading out right away, yet he had hoped he might have at least made a little headway.

No such luck. If anything, the gunfighters seemed even more stubborn and intractable than McQueen and Mariano – which was certainly going some.

This thinking was responsible for that heavy, hopeless feeling in the badgepacker's chest, for he'd hoped at least to bring about some lessening in the intensity of this murky war, yet now could only dread that its worst days might be ahead.

Brooding and scowling, the peace officer was only vaguely aware that the lights were still burning in Gail James's shop as he passed by. 'Suppose she's likely waitin' for Raybold to show up,' he mused glumly.

Which was precisely what Gail James was doing. But the girl was not the only one waiting for Raybold that summer's night. Standing virtually invisible in the darkened alley mouth across the broad street, Juan Mariano, who, like most other folks, knew Raybold and the girl were seeing one another, was doing the very same thing.

*

'Howdy, Duane.'

'Howdy do, Earl.'

They raised their glasses and drank. It was good bourbon which Earl Parnell had brought upstairs to Kitty Clare's room above the Big Wheel. Yet neither man drank with any sign of relish. This was their second drink since Raybold had arrived by the back stairs and their conversation had been punctuated by awkward silences, a situation unfamiliar to either man. Both were aware there was something amiss.

'Had a few words with our lawman,' Parnell said, in another effort to get things going following yet another of those awkward pauses. 'They tell me downstairs he was talkin' to you before I showed.'

Raybold smiled, but the smile didn't reach his eyes. 'Yeah, the badge suggested that it might be one good notion if you and me was to simply up and take our guns some place else.'

Parnell toyed with his glass, then looked up sharply. 'You figure he could be right, Duane?'

Raybold scowled. 'What do you mean?'

Parnell shrugged uncomfortably. Then he got up and moved around the little room, which, with its frilled curtains, scent of perfume and bright, gaudy clothing strewn around carelessly, accurately reflected the personality of its occupant.

'I got to be honest, pard,' he said finally. 'I don't like the game here.'

'You looking to pull out?' Raybold said sharply.

'Well . . . yeah, guess I am.'

'Then do it. You're a free agent.'

But Parnell shook his head. 'I don't mean on my own – I mean the both of us. This here set-up just isn't your style, Duane. Hell, a man can't always pick the right side, but at least most times you've been able to convince yourself you have. But this is different.'

The gunfighter paused to scratch the back of his head. 'Damnit, I feel like a Judas, Duane – damned if I don't. I mean that business today when the don got—'

'Why should you fret over whatever happens to Don Luis?' Raybold cut in. 'Mariano's never worried over a single soul but himself.'

'It ain't that, Duane. I reckon it's just the notion of you and me bein' on opposite sides.'

'We're not on opposite sides. Would we be here drinking together if we were?'

'I wish we were drinking together some place else, is all.'

Raybold got to his feet, a tall and impressive

figure in the lamplight.

'I'm not pulling out until I've finished what I came here to do, Earl. You're welcome to ride out any time you want. I could meet you somewheres else when all this is over and forgotten.'

For a long moment Earl Parnell considered doing just that. But only for a moment. For that was all the time he needed in order to recall all those other times – good times – when fighting shoulder-to-shoulder he and the man at his side now had righted plenty wrongs and sent many a badman killer to his rightful reward.

Parnell was no more sympathetic now towards what they were doing than had been the case at the beginning. Yet he knew then and there he wouldn't quit. Couldn't.

'Forget it, Duane,' he grinned. 'I'm stickin' with you. Come on, let's finish our shot.' He hefted his glass. 'Partners.'

'Partners,' Duane grunted. And drank deep.

CHAPTER 7

FRISCO STREET

Raybold was thoughtful as he walked down the long dim alleyway flanking the saloon, making for Frisco Street.

To Parsons and Parnell he had appeared quite intractable in their meetings tonight but in reality he was a lot less sure of himself than he appeared.

Yet this brief uncertainty had begun to recede by the time he hit Frisco Street where he paused to take a spell and to reflect some.

He was soon able to recall in detail that evil morning when he'd come into Whipple Creek toting his father's body . . . a lanky, ragged kid who couldn't fully comprehend what had taken place, yet who was plenty old enough to understand that something would have to be done about it.

But nothing was done.

It was as though his father had just happened to get shot down by some kind of accident.

He'd urged Parsons to round up McQueen and Don Luis and stand them up in court for murder. But all the lawman had done was advise him to go home and forget about it.

So why in hell should he fret about any innocents who might die here now? Nobody had fretted any over Charlie Raybold – that was for sure.

People made way for him as he headed for the dress shop, their wide eyes and whispers following his every step. Some he greeted by name and there was sober respect in their responses now. During his week back in Fort Such he'd renewed old acquaintances and established good relations with the influential citizens of the town. His natural charm backed up by his reputation made this easy enough. It seemed most of Fort Such looked upon him as a hero – the hometown boy who'd made good.

Sooner or later he meant to draw on this good-will. That was all part of his overall plan.

He was within sight of the dress shop when the voice halted him.

He turned to see Juan Mariano crossing the dusty street towards him. The young man's face was a deathly white in the lamplight and he wore a heavy double gunrig buckled low around the hips.

Raybold had automatically clapped hand to gun handle at his call. Now he deliberately let go of the weapon even though everything about this man – coming hard on the heels of what had transpired at Antigua that day – seemed to breathe danger.

Mariano halted a short distance away, right hand visibly shaking as it hovered over gun handle. 'I've come to finish you, Raybold!'

He spoke loudly and attracted wide-eyed specta-tors along both sides of the street. Raybold stood motionless before the window of the gunsmith's shop, eyes unblinking in the black shadow of his hat as they fixed the young aristocrat with a level stare.

And just as he remembered from earlier days, he felt the bite of old resentments and jealousy towards this Mariano – the boy who'd had every-thing while he'd had nothing.

What a prime chance to repay Don Luis in full measure for all the harm he'd done him!

He knew intuitively he could out-gun and kill this man left-handed. And nobody could after-wards claim he'd not been provoked or that he was guilty of anything other than simply reacting to save his own life.

But of course he knew he wouldn't do it. Could not.

Old habits died hard and one of the first strong habits he'd acquired in the gunfighting profession was never to take advantage of an inferior. Certainly he was being provoked and in some danger here, yet still knew he couldn't draw and shoot down Juan Mariano.

'You hear me, killer?' Mariano shouted, trying desperately to gear himself up for what he must do. 'You shot my father and now I'm going to shoot you. Draw your weapon!'

Raybold stepped down off the walk as a hushed street held its breath. Unhurriedly he walked towards the Mexican. Mariano first flushed then licked his lips. A moment later, he emitted a snarl and whipped into the draw.

The man got one shot away with the bullet tugging harmlessly at the shoulder padding of Raybold's jacket. Duane simply kept on with each step taking him swiftly closer. His air of total calm combined with the fact that he'd made no move towards his six-gun confused his adversary, causing him to delay just long enough for Raybold to reach him and snatch away the pistol.

'Damn you, gunfighter!' Mariano raged, angry at his own failure more than anything else. With a fierce curse he swung a punch which missed the target of the gunfighter's jaw by barely a whisper. Raybold responded with a vicious left hook which dropped the Mexican without a sound, sprawling on his back in the deep dust and out to the world.

Emptying the unfired weapon Raybold dropped it upon the man's chest and turned his back on him. By this a large mob had gathered. They were opening up before him just as a squad of angry Antigua riders with Earl Parnell at their head came storming into view. They didn't draw rein until reaching Raybold where he paused, solitary and calm, watching them.

'He-he's killed Juan, Parnell!' a *vaquero* shouted as Parnell leapt to ground. 'Take him down!'

'Juan's alive,' Raybold said quietly. 'Even if he

doesn't deserve to be.'

'Damn you, gunfighter!' Mariano raged, rising to his feet and rushing at him furiously. But Raybold swayed smoothly to one side and chopped a left hook hard to the jaw that dropped the man at his feet.

Parnell, white-faced and shaking, glared ferociously as he searched for words. 'Lucky for you that you didn't kill him, Raybold!'

The crowd waited tensely for Raybold's response, for as Sheriff Parsons had observed earlier that night, all this violence and bloodshed was merely whetting the public appetite for more. Right now there was scarcely a man present not expecting to witness a blazing showdown between two of the most intimidating men in the county.

They were doomed to disappointment. Raybold merely touched hat brim in acknowledgement of Parnell's words then walked off, tall and soberfaced through the parting throng to where Gail James stood waiting for him on the veranda of her shop.

By nature Curt August wasn't a man to fret over adversity. So it was that as that quiet Sabbath wore on he quietly took himself for a ride into the

Eternals where he planned on getting some clear thinking and forward planning done, well away from the confusion stemming from recent events, most of which had failed to go his way.

This calming exercise again proved successful. By the time he was heading back everything was once again clear in the mind of a highly dangerous man.

He saw plainly that if he was to retain his status as top gun of both Rancho Antigua and Pierro County he'd need to achieve three things fast.

The first would be to notch up a decisive triumph over Doubletree which would both lift his standing on Antigua and undercut Raybold's growing authority. The second was self-evident – get rid of Raybold himself – preferably the final, fatal way. With that accomplished then the final chore of eliminating Earl Parnell would prove simple and easy.

So he figured.

But first he must secure the don's approval – no mean feat due to the fact that Mariano had never liked him. But August was playing for keeps now and had done all his thinking and plotting before-hand, and so made a strong case when the don looked like proving difficult.

'I fear Doubletree might be strong enough to withstand any attack from us, Curt, and we already have—'

'I don't believe one word of that,' August cut in firmly. 'If we handle this right we can stage a surprise raid and bring McQueen to his knees in one hit. I've already set up a way to take Raybold out of the game before we strike. Doubletree is starting round-up at Two Mile Mesa in the middle of the week and they'll be needing plenty extra hands out there. I know that region well and I reckon if we play our cards right we'll make takin' out the guards at Whipple Creek and the Two Mile easy as winkin'.'

'I don't know ... what happened last night made me realize just how far this feud has gone. I might have already lost my own son, who knows? And what has a man left if he has no son to take over when he dies?'

'There's only one way to guarantee there'll still be a Rancho Antigua for Juan to inherit when and if you leave us, Don Luis, and that's to bring Doubletree to its knees right now.'

'All right damnit, Curt ... you handle it your way.'

'Thanks, *Patrón*,' August grinned, making for

108

the door. 'And don't fret. By this time next week McQueen will be beggin' for mercy, you'll see.'

Quitting the dark house August made for his cabin. He passed Parnell heading for the stables. As August hurried on his way Parnell halted to stare after him. August had actually grinned at him, and watching the tall, dark-garbed figure receding through the moonlight, Parnell frowned and massaged his rocky jaw.

'Now what's that sly gunshark up to? I swear I ain't seen him smile since the first day I rode in here.'

Libby was at the ranch house gate when she sighted the solitary horseman coming in from the direction of the mesa. Recognizing an opportunity, she swung the half-gate open and strolled down along the trail to greet the rider.

Raybold, looking just as relaxed as he had done when riding out at first light with the men heading for the mesa, reined in with a grin upon reaching her. He swung lightly down to walk beside her back towards headquarters.

'You look mighty fetching this evening, Miss Libby,' he said lightly. 'If you don't mind my saying so.'

She smiled at the compliment. 'Everything all right out at the mesa?'

'Sure. They're setting up camp today. The round-up will start in the morning.'

The girl halted as they approached the gate. 'Duane, there's something I've wanted to speak to you about.'

'Sure, thing. What?'

'It's about the other night. I haven't had the chance to thank you for what you did.'

'You mean Juan?'

Libby nodded. 'Yes. You spared his life.'

'I didn't spare the man, Libby. It's just that I didn't have to shoot him, is all.'

'I can't believe that.'

'It's so.'

'No. The hands told me how Juan shot at you. I was supervising the cleaning of your room yesterday and I found your coat – the one with a bullet hole under the armpit. So, I know it was true . . . what they said.'

Raybold frowned. 'The man was shaking like a jelly falling down steps. I knew I was pretty safe.'

'I don't believe any of that, Duane Raybold. Now, this might sound foolish but I have a strong feeling that you did what you did, for me. You knew what it would do to me if anything happened to Juan, and—'

'You're free to believe whatever you like, Libby,' he cut in soberly, moving away. 'But the big reason I didn't shoot Mariano was that I didn't have to. If you believe anything else then you're wrong.'

He walked on. The girl didn't follow. Reaching the gate Raybold halted and called back. 'And cut out that moonlighting with Mariano, will you? I asked you to do that before, but I know you were out again last night. Now I've warned the boys not to let you through again.'

Libby lifted her chin defiantly. 'They'll let me through. They'd do anything for me.'

He quit arguing. No point. For he knew what she said to be so. And making his thoughtful way uphill for the house he told himself he was right in not wanting her to be seeing that man while conceding at the same time he could not forbid it. Love would always find a way, even in battle-scarred Pierro County – but that worn platitude didn't make him feel one whit better about it all.

McQueen was at work in the den when the gun-fighter entered the house. The rancher set down his pen and looked up in surprise.

'Anythin' wrong, Duane? You look kind of edgy.'

Raybold placed his hat upon the desk carefully and sat down, shaking his head.

'Everything's fine at the mesa, Ben. I just came by to make sure things were the same here.'

'Yeah . . . all quiet, Duane.' The rancher leaned back and locked big hands behind his head. 'But I can't quite make up my mind if that's good or bad. Seems to me Antigua's been mighty quiet all over these past few days. Got any notions why that should be so?'

'Nope,' Raybold lied.

He knew well enough. Too well.

He realized his presence was responsible for the fact that there had been no significant clashes between the two big spreads since Saturday. But the reason for this wasn't, as McQueen might suspect, because Antigua was busy licking its wounds. Raybold was leading up to a massive final clash between the powerful spreads and, while making his plans, was content to let things run a quiet course. And with Parnell acting upon his orders in the Antigua camp this had proved easy enough to achieve.

'Well, I got me a feelin' that Antigua's been worse hurt than we figured, Duane,' McQueen confessed after a pause. 'And so I reckon it's time we struck again. Matter of fact, I've been waitin' on you to come up with somethin'.'

'You got anything special in mind, Ben?'

'Why, nothin' really special as such, Duane. I want to just go on houndin' Mariano until he's ground right down there into the dust, that's all.'

'You really hate him, don't you, Ben?'

'That greaser upstart!'McQueen snarled explosively. 'Sure I hate him. I hate all them Mexes with their high and mighty ways.'

He paused, instantly changed the subject.

'Libby was off ridin' again some place last night, Duane. I got a hunch she's still seein' young Mariano. You know anythin' about that?'

Raybold met the rancher's stare levelly. 'No.'

'Hmm,' the man muttered. 'I don't know if I believe you or not. That there girl's been able to twist every man on this spread around her finger for years on end and I'm not sure she couldn't still do it right now if she wanted.'

'I don't hear anything about her seeing Mariano.'

'OK, we'll leave it go at that. But of course the only way to prevent anythin' like that is simple – get rid of the greasers once and for all.' Hard blue eyes stabbed at Raybold. 'We've been too quiet too

113

long, Duane. I want some action.'

Raybold held up a hand. 'Just be patient a couple of days longer, Ben. I'm working on something.'

'You are?' McQueen was eager. Over ten days he'd come to rely heavily on the other's ability and judgement. 'What?'

'A big raid,' Raybold told him, crossing long legs and taking out a cigar. 'The biggest yet as a matter of fact.'

This was the truth, or at least a half-truth. For the reality was that Raybold was planning a massive attack upon Rancho Antigua. But what McQueen didn't know, or even begin to guess, was that Raybold, through Parnell, planned to make certain Antigua was expecting them.

He was plotting a full-scale head-on clash designed to cripple both giants, weakening them to such a degree that the third force in Pierro County – something that neither McQueen nor Mariano knew existed – would then be able under his leadership to move in and administer the final coup and at last bring peace. With honour.

Ben McQueen rubbed big leathery palms together with a dry papery sound.

'Now, that's the sort of talk I like to hear, Duane.

So – what are we waitin' for? Why don't we get right on with it? Don't you fret none about the round-up. Hell, I'd be willing to miss round-up altogether this season if it meant—'

'Don't worry, I don't plan to delay too long,' Raybold reassured him. He was experiencing that powerful thick feeling in the back of his throat that came with the prospect of vengeance approaching its final bloody hour. 'I'm just as eager to get this over and done with as you are, Ben.'

McQueen was so enlivened by this he offered Raybold a drink, a courtesy normally never accorded hired help. Raybold, who always drank sparingly, and never when actually working, declined with the excuse he was heading back to the mesa.

'So . . . not goin' into town tonight?' McQueen sounded surprised as they moved out on to the gallery. He nudged the gunfighter and winked elaborately. 'Not itchin' to go-see if they got any hot bargains at the dress shop?'

'Not tonight,' Raybold replied soberly, frowning as he looked south where the high rim of Two Mile Mesa thrust into the sunset sky.

Catching his glance, McQueen turned sober. 'You're not worried about nothin' are you?'

115

'Not exactly worried. But like you say, Antigua's been just a mite too quiet the past couple of days, seems to me. They just could be buildin' up to something.'

This made sense to Ben McQueen even though it was not the real reason behind Raybold's edgy vigilance. At their meeting at Whipple Creek the previous night, Earl had reported how Curt August had been acting a little strangely over recent days. Parnell had the notion August might be up to something unlikely to prove to be any good for either himself or Doubletree.

Upon taking his departure from McQueen, Raybold headed downslope to the stables where the hostler unsaddled his black then cut him out a reliable mount for the night's work ahead.

That done Duane made for the cookshack. Later he was just attacking an inch-thick steak when he heard a rider approaching headquarters from the direction of the town trail.

Getting up, he went to the window. The rider, now loping into view past the stables, was Fort Such's resident drunk, philosopher and general mischief-maker, Mick Clayton. The man's hired mount was well-lathered and looked as though it might have been galloped all the way.

116

'Hi, Mick!' he called from the door. 'What you doing out here?'

'Ah, there you are, Duane. The West's fastest and California's finest!'

Raybold was frowning as he came down the steps. 'You drunk again, Mick?'

'Alas, if only that were so, friend Raybold,' Clayton sighed. 'For I fear I am the bearer of ill tidings. There was an unseemly incident in Fort Such during which the shop and effects of Miss Gail James were somewhat damaged and disarrayed by—'

'Gail?' Raybold rapped, seizing the headstall of Clayton's horse. 'In plain English, man – what happened?'

Clayton straightened and talked fast.

'A couple of bums started a ruckus in her shop an hour or so ago. Seems they were drunk and got out of hand. Knocked the shop around and gave that little girl a few bruises, so they did. I figured considering your, er, friendship with the young lady, that bringing this news to you might earn a man a small gratuity, perhaps?'

'Here!' Raybold rapped, snapping a five-dollar bill from a shirt pocket. And before a gaping Clayton could thank him, was running for the stables.

117

He was soon out on the trail for Fort Such after quitting Doubletree at the gallop. He settled down to a steadier pace, then held to it every mile to his destination.

CHAPTER 8

IN OLD FORT SUCH

The ride to Fort Such was uneventful and swift. Upon his arrival Duane was relieved to find Gail's injuries were no worse than minor. Indeed he found her back at work in the dress shop repairing the damage caused by the saddle tramps. She insisted that all she needed to assist her full recovery was a hearty meal – and would he stay for supper?

She found herself forced to repeat her invitation; Raybold was staring fixedly at the bruises on her arm left there by the two roughnecks.

'Sorry – got to get back to the spread,' he lied.

119

Then added casually, 'What did this pair look like, Gail?'

'Well, rough, dirty and mean—' She broke off sharply. 'Duane, you're not considering—?'

He didn't hear the rest as he studied her with a strange intensity. He was now coming to realize with a jolt just how much this woman and her safety had come to mean. And thought – all those years he'd kept love at bay until now when it had plainly sneaked in under his guard!

Yet in the very next moment he was back to reality and reminding himself fiercely, *Great, maybe, but not for you, gunfighter.* And so quickly turned to go, leaving her with a big fake smile and a promise to call back real soon.

He went directly to the sheriff's office to find Parsons sipping cold coffee from a cracked mug. The man looked up and seemed to comprehend everything at a glance like he was reading clear newsprint.

'Don't tell me – let me guess, son. And the answer's no. I'm not telling you anything about that pair who roughed up your fine little lady.' He slugged down some coffee and belched. 'Anythin' else?'

Raybold reasoned and threatened to no avail

before finally storming out. Slamming a fist into his palm with a hard smacking sound, he went striding off down Union Street until he came upon a knot of citizens on the walk, whom he promptly quizzed regarding the saddle tramps. Only one recalled the pair but knew nothing beyond that.

It wasn't until he buttonholed Kitty Clare at the Big Wheel and furnished that boozy madam with good descriptions of the pair that he struck it lucky.

'Oh, them two beauties, eh?' She nodded, taking a swig of bourbon from a pitcher. She burped in a lady-like way. 'Sure they was hangin' around some. So – what about 'em, honey-chile?' She paused, squinting at him closely. 'Oh-oh, I know that look of yours, Duane Raybold, and it means trouble. Well, I ain't a-tellin' you no more about any low bums than I—'

She broke off mid-sentence. He was holding a five-dollar bill between his fingers. Kitty Clare licked glossy red lips like she was tasting imported French wine. But again she frowned, shook her head and made a dismissive gesture as though banishing temptation.

'Duane Raybold!' she chided. 'You got no right temptin' me when I know by that look in your eye you is gonna hurt somebody or throw 'em in the caboose for fifty years or—'

She fell silent as he reached out as though to reclaim his five-spot from its nestling place between her two finest features. She seized his hand and hissed, 'All right, damnit! Bailey's Rooming House on Pacific Street, you evil man! But just remember I never told you nothin'. If those tough *hombres* get the jump on you and beat you up and make you start talkin'—'

She broke off for Raybold was already gone, striding away down a wind-blowing street to a corner where a creaking sign hanging over a grimy saloon porch read boldly: GIRLS – WHISKEY – MORE GIRLS! and stepped inside.

The bartender scented trouble on him at a glance.

The barman told himself he was not afraid. But he was having big trouble at home with a woman who was bigger and tougher than he was and, apart from that, he didn't feel like riling this tall pilgrim by lying to him. So he just inclined his head eloquently in the direction of a parlour door then waited for the next customer whom he hoped might simply be interested in such things as girls or whiskey. Not trouble.

'Sure, Mr Raybold, sir,' bartender Bailey said after the tall stranger had stated his business. 'Them two pilgrims you describe were stayin' here, right enough. I never knew it was them what roughed up that pretty gal. But I'm afraid you're a bit late. They hauled their freight two hours back.'

It was disappointing but Raybold wasn't ready to quit. So he set off on another round of dives, dumps and even a few semi-respectable joints until winding up in a squalid dive named Mario's down at the gloomy southern end of Frisco Street where he spotted a busted-nose waddy swigging tequila while attempting to romance a slatternly Mexican serving girl.

He hailed a passing waiter who knew everybody in town, even the passers-through. Turned out he knew Busted-Nose's real handle was Chot Kirk.

Oblivious of trouble closing in from behind, Chot Kirk was spinning the three-time-loser a tired old line about how rich he was and how beautiful she was – even if she might be pushing forty-five uphill.

The hardcase's sugary words were chopped off as a gunbarrel smashed down upon the bar, causing him to jump a foot. He howled in rage and came up out of his chair like a wild animal only to confront a tall, cold-faced stranger holding a gun and staring him straight in the eye.

Kirk grabbed for his sneak gun, then froze. There was something about this stranger that chilled. He sensed the newcomer was hoping he might grab his gun up again just so he could blow his brains out.

'Mr Raybold!' gasped the bartender. 'Is something the matter?'

'Raybold?' Chot Kirk groaned. He'd heard enough about that one to cause him to snatch his hand off gunbutt like it was suddenly white-hot.

'Get on to your feet and use that gun!' the gunfighter hissed in his face.

'I-I never knew that gal meant anythin' to you, Raybold. D-don't kill a man . . . I never meant nothin'. It ain't me what you wanna even scores with . . . it's the feller what put me up to it that you oughta be huntin'.'

Raybold frowned. 'What'd you say . . . what feller?'

'Why, Antigua's gunfighter – Curt August.'

'August? Why, you lying—'

'No, I ain't lyin', Raybold. I'm tellin' you. August fronted us last night and gave us ten bucks apiece to rough up that gal and wreck her place.'

Raybold hesitated. Kirk was plainly scared, and sounded like he was telling the truth. But why would August pull a caper like that?

The answer struck like a lightning bolt. To get him away from Doubletree, of course! That had to be it.

Raybold whirled and was gone in moments to leg it fast to the Big Wheel where he swung astride the first tethered horse he came to and roared down Frisco Street at the gallop.

Parnell and the Antigua hands were just sitting down to supper at the cookshack when August came jingling in. 'All right, you bindle-stiffs!' he bawled. 'Get up and get saddled. We're ridin' on Doubletree!'

In the stunned silence every eye cut to Parnell, something not lost on the envious August.

'You likkered up, August?' Parnell queried.

August ignored the remark. 'We're ridin' on Doubletree, Mister Parnell. Don Luis's orders.'

'But I heard the don was against a raid?'

'Against a big raid, yeah. But the way I've planned this, there ain't gonna be no risks. All right, the rest of you, stop gawkin' and go get your guns.'

The men turned uncertainly to Parnell, who obligingly did the talking for them. 'You sure this is what the don wants, August?'

'If it'll steady your butterflies, hero,' August sneered, 'I staged a caper to draw Raybold off to Fort Such. There's a passel of men at the Two Mile just waitin' to eat our lead right now.' He tilted his hat forward over one eye. 'So, let's hustle!'

In their saddles within minutes the cowboy-gunmen rode out with confidence in August and Parnell and intent on settling old scores. Twenty minutes later the glow of campfire lights alerted them that the enemy was relaxing and unsuspecting – sitting ducks in gunpacker parlance.

'It's Antigua – mow them down!' Doubletree ramrod Olan Pike roared in his booming voice, and next moment the night was shattered by the roar of guns.

August led the charge and in mere moments the hillside became a beehive of running and shooting men – the wide-awake and murderously intent cowboy faction versus the stumbling, shouting and eventually wildly shooting enemy. The distance was still too great for accuracy, but it was closing fast and men were already falling on either side. August led his attack without fear, while in the trees Parnell and the hand-picked Antigua men watched the ever-widening clash in taut silence – biding their time until counter-attacking.

This was total war . . . and only the bravest and luckiest would survive.

Raybold rode directly for Two Mile Mesa, travelling swiftly astride a borrowed mount.

But even then he was too late. He realized this when within a half-mile of Two Mile Mesa, he caught the first whiff of gunsmoke. From a short distance further on came the cry of a badly wounded man. Another fifty yards' distance and the campsite leapt into view.

Raybold reined up with a jerk.

The scene spreading before him was a grim and smoke-fogged landscape with bodies sprawled carelessly in death and the sounds of men in pain and fear mingling with the stink of gunsmoke. Then abruptly came a challenging shout from a nearby clump of aspen.

'Who in hell is that?'

'Raybold!' he hollered back, reining up just long enough to be identified before heeling the lathered animal forward again.

He rode past the dead. He identified some: Tom

Junee, Billy Joe Wilkes, Gun-shy Martin, Murch Rogan and Shep Willis. . . .

He'd numbered seven by the time he reached the camp where Olan Pike and other survivors were attending their wounded.

Swinging down he tried to convince himself this was what he'd wanted to happen. So – August had tricked him tonight. But what did that matter as long as the results were there? This had to be seen as a mortal blow against McQueen. If Duane could achieve a similar strike against Antigua, then his full vengeance would be that much closer to realization.

Yet try as he might Raybold failed to feel his spirits lift any as he moved along and even began to feel that fierce resolve that had driven him for so long begin to weaken.

Rancho Antigua and Doubletree were not just names or numbers – chessmen on a board. You couldn't cancel knights and pawns in this game without shedding blood.

A weary and grey-faced Pike eventually reported what had taken place: August had lured them into a trap and they'd tumbled into it. There were more dead than Raybold wanted to think about on both sides.

With a major effort he shook himself into action and assisted with the wounded for a spell before mounting up and heading for town. He rode staring straight ahead, ignoring half-seen scenes of violence and blood before he accidentally came upon yet another dead man sprawled in the grass with two weary looking cowboys standing nearby.

'Been back-shot, Duane,' gangling Corey Johnson called. 'They musta got him from that clump of aspen yonder.'

Duane made no response. He was fighting the ugly suspicion that there was something familiar about that blood-soaked striped shirt as he stepped to ground.

'Turn him over.' His voice sounded dry as dust.

The cowboy shrugged but did as ordered. It would be a long time before he'd forget the look on Duane Raybold's face when he stared down into the sightless eyes of Earl Parnell.

CHAPTER 9

FALLEN IDOL

'You say Raybold's holdin' a meetin' at the Big Wheel?' Sheriff Parsons rumbled, raising his weary head from his hands. 'What sort of a meetin'?'

Buck Channing, the liveryman who'd brought the bad news to the jailhouse, looked troubled. 'Maybe you'd better come along and see for yourself, Sheriff.'

Sheriff Parsons was tempted to tell Channing to go straight to hell. It was the evening of one of the longest days the badge-toter could recall. A day in which Fort Such had been occupied almost totally with the laying to rest of men slain out on

130

Doubletree the previous night. Yet tired, disillusioned and bitter though he might be, Parsons was still the dutiful lawman.

'All right, Buck,' he sighed. 'I'll be along in a minute.'

Channing went out leaving Parsons staring bleakly at the door. Mustering his flagging energy the peace officer eventually made it to his feet, picked up his hat and followed.

'And we *are* strong enough,' so Raybold was declaring when the lawman entered the Big Wheel a short time later. 'I reckon we could muster a fighting force of fifty guns which should be sufficient to overcome Doubletree and Antigua—'

'What's he spoutin' about?' Parsons demanded of drunk Mick Clayton. 'Did he say he's fixin' to ride on Doubletree and Antigua?'

The man replied eagerly. 'Sure as shootin', Sheriff.' But his words were drowned by Raybold as he launched into a spirited account of all that had gone wrong and how he figured it could best be made right.

A cheer, uncertain at first yet quickly growing in volume, greeted his words. By the time the racket had died down, an angry Sheriff Parsons had reached the dais.

'What's the meanin' of this uproar, Raybold?' he demanded. 'Hasn't there been enough killin' to satisfy you?'

Raybold responded angrily and the uproar continued until Parsons got up on stage and bellowed for quiet. He spoke soberly and convincingly; 'I understand your feelin's, boys, but before you go off half-cocked it would be best if you knew why he's been so keen to lead you.'

'I just told them,' Raybold stated.

'I'm not so sure of that. You sure you're not just out to even the score for what happened to your pard, Parnell?'

'That's not the reason. But if it was I'd have the right to revenge.' Raybold turned to the mob again to deliver a brief but effective response that ended with the words, 'And as a fellow citizen and fellow victim like all you folks, I'm asking every man who's got the guts to ride with me to lift his hand!'

The minutes that followed this were chaotic but it soon became plain that Raybold, the gunfighter-hero, was winning the mob over. This drove the lawman to object again, only to be quickly drowned out by the worked-up throng.

'You don't gotta ride with us if you ain't willin'.

We can handle this easy, can't we, Raybold?'

'Do it *damned* easy!' Raybold hollered back, leaping down off the stage. 'So let's get to it now!'

'Stop!'

Few heard the cry but all saw Kitty Clare mount the dais. Garbed all in black from the funeral, her prettily powdered face now red and swollen from weeping, the girl extended her arms for quiet.

'Whatever you got to say will have to wait, Kitty!' Raybold barked. 'We got work to do.'

'Killing, don't you mean?' she retorted.

'Call it what you crave, gal,' he retorted as he made for the steps. But the girl's voice halted him.

'You can't bring Earl back, Duane.'

Raybold turned sharply. It took him a moment to find his voice. 'I know that. But I'm not doing this for myself but for these good folks.'

Kitty shook her head. 'Not so. And if you don't stop this foolishness, Duane, I'll tell them the real reason you came to Fort Such in the first place.'

It was suddenly still with every eye now focused upon Duane Raybold.

'Just what do you mean by that, Kitty?' he said.

'I don't want to have to tell them, Duane. And I shan't if you promise there'll be no more shooting.'

133

'Damnit! Don't you want to see Earl avenged?'

Kitty shook her head. 'I'm just a saloon girl but I'm smart enough to know that an eye for an eye never achieves anything—'

'Just a minute, girl,' Parsons cut in. 'What was that about the *real* reason for Duane coming here?'

The girl stared at Raybold. 'Don't force me to tell, Duane.'

'I don't know what you're talking about, Kitty.'

'I'm not bluffing, Duane. Earl told me the true story . . . and you're forcing me to tell it now. . . .'

He made no response and the girl turned to the mob to address them in a cool, controlled voice.

'Everybody . . . you're all ready to follow Duane tonight, I can see. But before you do anything you should know the truth. Duane is not really interested in any of you, any more than he's interested in bringing law and order to Pierro County. All he wants is to destroy Doubletree and Rancho Antigua in revenge for what happened to his father seven years ago.'

'That's a lie!' the gunfighter snarled.

'Is it, Duane?' she challenged. 'Can you deny you and Earl were working together to bring Doubletree and Rancho Antigua down?'

'Damned right I can,' Raybold said hotly. 'Don't

134

listen to her. It's all lies.'

'Duane,' Kitty pleaded, 'think of what you're doing. By denying the truth you are accusing Earl of being a liar – yet Earl is dead now and can't defend himself.'

Raybold glared balefully at the girl for almost a minute, emotions warring with one another in his face. Finally, he said, 'All damned right – so what if it *is* so? That doesn't—'

His voice was drowned out by the disbelieving gasp welling up from the mob. But these faces were no longer admiring as somebody shouted hoarsely, 'You mean you admit you was lyin' to us, Raybold?'

'Is it true you just come back to Fort Such to stir up this here feud again?' challenged another.

A bottle landed upon the stage with a splintering crash as angry emotion gripped the mob. Raybold realized he'd lost them. Outwardly calm yet intimidating, he drew the twin white-handled six-guns and stepped down from the dais to make his way unhurriedly to the rear door which he passed on through unchecked.

This whole deal had played against him, he brooded, as he trudged along the back streets towards Mario's a short time later. His gaze sought out that little hill on the south side of town where he'd lain Earl to rest, and slowly the emotion drained from his face. What had Earl said? '*This isn't our style, Duane. It's all wrong, man. . . .*'

And now, despite those seven years in which dreams of revenge had dominated his existence, Duane Raybold sensed that the bloody saga of revenge was drawing to a close and that Earl's death had been his punishment.

All those men dead because of him. . . .

Then came memories of his father and the bitter vow he'd made. He couldn't weaken now. Would not. Tomorrow he would be able to think clearly again. Tonight, right now, he only needed oblivion.

Raybold blinked at the sound of a voice at his elbow, turned to stare uncomprehendingly into the face that had appeared at his side in the dim light of the saloon.

'Why, Duane?' the girl asked calmly. 'Why would you want to do a thing like this?'

'I've got my reasons.'

'It's something to do with your father, isn't it?'

He stared. 'How in hell did you know that?'

'I'm right, aren't I?'

136

'Maybe.'

'Your face alters whenever your pa is mentioned, Duane. And it was only when I heard what happened at the Big Wheel tonight that I felt I understood the reason behind what you've been doing. You hold Ben McQueen and Don Luis responsible for what happened to your father, don't you? Poor Duane. Nursing your hate all those years.'

'And wouldn't you hate too, Gail? Hate like hell if your father had been murdered like—'

'He wasn't murdered.'

Raybold stared. '*What?*'

'The night your father was killed he'd stolen cows off Doubletree. The hands chased him before running into a bunch of Antigua riders hunting for some of their cows your father had also stolen. It was—'

'You're saying Pa was a thief, Gail?'

'He *was* a thief. And he was killed when he was caught stealing cows.'

'I don't believe that. I won't!'

'You were still a boy and you'd just lost your father, so Sheriff Parsons felt you had enough to bear without adding to it by burdening you with the truth.'

'Parsons?'

Gail nodded. 'I was only thirteen and knew no more than you did. But I know it's all true. If your father hadn't been killed in that clash he would have been hanged for rustling.'

Raybold couldn't believe it. But meeting the girl's level stare, how could he deny it?

She spoke softly now. 'I'm only telling you all this because I feel I had to, for your sake.'

Raybold rose to his feet, ashen-faced. 'Not true,' he muttered. 'Can't be. . . .'

But inside he sensed it just might be so. And when the girl offered to show him the record books at the jailhouse which would prove her words, he waited only for a moment before grunting; 'OK, let's do it.'

Parsons was preparing to lock up when the pair entered the jailhouse a half-hour later. It was Gail who calmly explained why they'd come, and the badgepacker sighed. Yet he willingly produced his charge book which covered many years and contained detailed charges lodged against Duane's father.

The clincher was an account of the night Charlie Raybold lost his life. An entry by Parsons supported by sworn statements signed by

McQueen and several of his riders revealed they had ridden to Whipple Creek on the night in question to retrieve seven head of cattle run off by Charlie Raybold. And that said it all.

'I'm sorry, Duane,' Gail commiserated. 'But you had to know. . . .'

He couldn't argue with that. Right now he could neither think nor speak.

It was several hours later as he walked the night streets of Fort Such before Raybold could grasp it all and eventually accept the fact his father had been a common thief.

He was walking away from the graveyard just as the Eternals were beginning to emerge from night's grip. Out there lay Doubletree and Antigua where men who, partly because of his actions, were now locked in a struggle to the death.

Suddenly that understanding became a huge burden of responsibility to carry – and in this same moment Duane Raybold clearly knew what he must do.

There was only one way in which he could balance out the scales, he knew, as he quit the cemetery and headed purposefully back towards the sleeping town.

Ben McQueen was in a foul temper and the news
Olan Pike brought him that morning wasn't calculated to soothe him any.

'Raybold to see you, boss.'

'Raybold?' he echoed. 'That bastard wouldn't
durst show his Judas face hereabouts if—'

'Pa,' broke in Libby, rising from the breakfast
table. 'Control your temper, please!'

'Good advice, Libby,' said a voice from the
doorway. And Raybold walked in.

'Pike!' roared McQueen. 'Shoot him!'

Suddenly everyone was shouting at once.

'Everybody shut up,' McQueen bawled. 'Pike,
didn't I give you an order?'

'Before we get to shooting, Ben,' Raybold cut in,
'I've got a few facts you should hear.'

McQueen continued ranting before Libby eventually managed to calm him some.

'For heaven's sake, Pa! At least hear what Duane
has to say, can't you?'

'All right, all goddamn right!' the rancher sput-
tered, somehow getting his emotions under
control. 'So, talk, blast you, Raybold. *Then* I'll
shoot you!'

'You've got a right to be sore,' Raybold conceded. 'But hear me out. You see, I always held you and Don Luis responsible for what happened to my pa and it was only last night I found out the truth.'

'What? That old Charlie was a thief?' McQueen snarled.

Raybold looked pale. 'Right.' He glanced at Libby, then continued. 'I planned for seven years to come back here and get square with you, old man. But now, and with what I know, I mean to heal what damage I've done. I want to bury the hatchet and make my peace with you.'

'Bury the hatchet?' McQueen bellowed, then went diving for the .45 on a nearby bench. But his daughter got there before him and hurled the weapon through a window in a shower of shimmering glass shards. Defiantly then she stood in front of Raybold and spread her arms wide protectively.

'Not another trantrum, Pa!' she defied him. 'You know Doubletree is on its knees after all that's happened. We don't even have the strength to fight Antigua any more, let alone half the county. Please—'

The old man suddenly began to cough. His fea-

141

tures reddened and he was swaying alarmingly when the girl ran to him and led him to a chair, forcing him to sit. Coughing and cursing, McQueen was plainly in no shape to spit, much less wage war. He eventually seemed to realize this as he allowed his daughter to pat down his hair and soothingly call him 'Poppa' from her childhood days.

'Please listen to whatever Duane has to say,' she begged. 'Couldn't you just grab this chance to make peace with Don Luis? Surely there's been enough killing to last you both for what you have left of your lifetimes?'

A long silence. Then Olan Pike spoke up. 'Could be she's likely right, boss. We ain't got enough men these days to ride herd on the beeves, much less do much of anythin' else.'

Chagrined, red-faced and breathing like a bellows, the rancher fought a bitter internal battle before he was able to speak and make sense – of a kind. 'How the hell do we know Mariano would want to talk treaty even if I agreed?' he challenged Raybold. 'You been to see him?'

'Sure thing,' Duane lied smoothly. But it was really only half a lie, for a Mariano rider had quietly told him his boss man was actually ready to

talk a deal. Both these powerful and arrogant cat-
tlemen had grown old and weary from fighting
one another and only needed to acknowledge that
fact now – or so he believed.

There followed any amount of heated argument, posturing and fierce debate. Yet in the end
most everybody heaved a sigh of relief when the
red-faced rancher turned to stare at Duane long
and balefully in silence before speaking gruffly. 'I
guess it took a fair bit of grit for you to come see
me this way, huh?'

'Not half as much as you'll show if you give the
nod to sitting down and talking.'

'All right, dad-blast it!' McQueen snorted, grind-
ing his teeth as he turned away. 'I'll talk if that
horse's rump will too . . . so what are you waitin'
for? Get the hell off my place, I got work to do and
men loafin' about and gettin' paid, goddamnit!'

Strolling for the gates with the girl a short time
later, Raybold still couldn't quite believe he'd
pulled it off – or close enough to it.

'Thanks heaps for backing my play, Libby. I
couldn't have done it without you chiming in. I'm
not sure why you did.'

'Well, you really should know by this, Duane
Raybold. You spared Juan's life the other night so

it was the least I could do to intercede here. In any case, I believe the don and Father are both heartily sick of this eternal fighting, though neither would have ever agreed to talking peace if you hadn't shamed them into it.'

'I hope you're right ... about the peace, I mean.'

'I am,' she smiled with all the confidence and assurance of the young. She took his hand. 'Come on, I'll walk you to your horse.'

CHAPTER 10

THE GUNS
NO MORE

Vaquero Juan Paulo started in shock as Raybold came riding up abruptly from out of the tall grass. The *vaquero* grabbed hold of his Colt .44, then let go of it in panic. He made to gallop away but changed his mind yet again.

'Make sure you keep a sharp eye out up here,' they'd warned when posting him up here in the Eternals. But they'd clean forgotten to tell him what to do should he come face to face with Duane Raybold.

'Take it easy, cowboy!' Raybold called calmingly. He spread empty hands. 'See? I'm not geared for trouble.'

'W-what do you want here, Raybold? There is nothing here for y—'

'Is Don Luis at the house?'

'*Sí.*'

'Then I'm here to see him.'

The *vaquero* was only partly reassured. His gaze swept the empty low hills beyond Raybold suspiciously and there was a cold sweat on his brow.

'I said it's all right,' Raybold growled. 'I'm on my own . . . if you want to ride in with me.' He almost smiled. 'That might look good to your boss?'

Not waiting for a response Raybold turned his prad and loped off down-trail towards the Antigua acres. Realizing he had little option now, the scared Mexican booted his pony in the ribs and followed.

The pair encountered another two herders a half-mile further on, creating more alarm. But once reassured the gunfighter had come in alone, these two also quit their posts and rode in with them.

Something big was plainly afoot and they didn't want to miss any of it.

146

Their arrival at Rancho Antigua headquarters caused an uproar, and one jittery house boy actually squeezed off a wild shot in Raybold's direction before another angrily disarmed him and waved the riders in.

'You must forgive my young *compañero*, Raybold,' Palo said with a grin as they headed for the impressive hacienda. Then the smile faded instantly. 'Besides, if there is any killing to be done today, that task shall fall to me.'

Raybold scarcely heard. He was too busy scanning the no man's land of the Antigua stronghold. Don Luis and Juan had appeared on the shadowed portico of the hacienda while armed hands were coming in from all over. There was no sign of Curt August, for which he was grateful. When he enquired after the fast gun, his escort simply shrugged.

'Who knows, *señor*? Perhaps he is in town, perhaps in the mountains. One rarely knows where the Señor August goes.'

Then suddenly, 'What is the meaning of this?' Juan Mariano challenged from the broad stone steps of the gallery as the cavalcade came to a halt before him. 'Have you gone crazy?'

Fingering hat back from forehead, Raybold took

his time replying. 'Could be . . . but I doubt it.' He gazed past Mariano to where the don stood, imposing and aloof. 'Do I have your permission to step down, Don Luis?'

The don, pale from his wound and leaning upon a cane, frowned faintly.

'You are not welcome at this place, Señor Raybold.' He touched his side. 'Perhaps you have already forgotten you attempted to kill me but days ago?'

'You may not believe this, *señor*, but I shot to warn that day, not kill.'

'As you said – I may not believe you. From what I hear you are a man not to be trusted, *señor*.'

'You've heard about last night, then?'

'Yes, we heard, Raybold,' Juan interjected, face cold and white with anger. 'By the very Virgin I don't know what—'

'We can swap fighting talk until dark-down if you want, mister,' Raybold cut in. 'But that's not what I came here for.' He turned back to the don. 'Might we talk inside, Don Luis?'

The *ranchero* hesitated for a moment, then sighed with weighty reluctance. 'Very well, if you wish, although I fail to see what might be gained.'

But several short minutes later in the privacy of

the plush front parlour, both the don and Juan were absorbed by the time the gunfighter had informed of his visit to Doubletree earlier that morning.

'You say McQueen wishes to talk peace?' Juan said disbelievingly. 'But – how could this be?'

'I figure Ben McQueen's realized that nobody can win a feud – or at least not a feud like this one,' Raybold stated, standing straight in the centre of this richly-furnished room. 'He took a pretty bad mauling the other night at Two Mile Mesa and—'

'So, that is the reason, is it?' Don Luis cut in, seating himself behind a polished hardwood table. 'When the gringo realizes he has been defeated he cravenly seeks to sue for peace.'

'The decision to try to talk peace wasn't Ben's, but mine, Don Luis.'

'Yours?' Juan said disbelievingly. 'After what we heard last night you expect us to believe now that you wish to bring us together?'

Raybold remained cool and clear-spoken as he revealed the reason why he had played the role he had chosen in the feud, and why he'd finally abandoned it.

The Marianos heard him out in silence. When he was finally through, father and son traded puzzled glances before the elder man spoke.

'Perhaps I could believe you, Señor Raybold, and perhaps I might even understand what you have done. But what you ask today is impossible. There can be no peace between Rancho Antigua and Doubletree. This feud is of Ben McQueen's making and for the first time Antigua has gained the upper hand.'

'Not really, Don Luis,' Raybold countered soberly. 'You and Doubletree are still too alike in strength for either one to win a fight outright. Slowly but surely Doubletree would regain its full power . . . and things would again be just as they have been – for forever it would seem—'

'Do you believe I want this war?' stormed Don Luis, bringing down his fist upon the polished table. 'I do not, Señor Raybold. But there can be no peace. Ben McQueen hates all Mexicans – he has stated so publicly a hundred times in the past.'

'Don't lay it all at McQueen's feet, Don Luis. You can't deny you hate him equally, and maybe all gringos.' He raised a hand as Mariano made to interject. 'But it doesn't really signify if that is so or not. All you have to do is admit there have been faults on both sides and I reckon we could all be halfway to peace right now – maybe even today.'

Following a long and weighty silence, Juan turned to gaze thoughtfully at his father. 'Perhaps Raybold is right? Perhaps it really is time to forget all the hatred and sue for peace?'

Don Luis tugged at his little beard as he chewed on the big question. Did he really want peace? Did he have it in his heart to forgive Ben McQueen?

He was still wrestling with this when a shadow flitted through the doorway and Curt August stood there, his smile like ice.

'So . . . face to face at last, Raybold!'

Moving away from the table to confront the new danger, Raybold said, 'I'm not here to make trouble, August.'

'Well, that surely is somethin' to know – like hell!'

'We're considering a truce, Curt,' Don Luis said.

'Well, ain't that just dandy.' August spat a curse. 'You can't be serious?'

Mariano rose uneasily. 'Now, Curt, this is no time for angry words – or guns.'

'The hell you say!' August was riding a lightning bolt of rage. He'd made his big plans in the Eternals that involved a smashing victory over Doubletree, Parnell out of the way, Raybold dead. And with one quick shot it could all be in his grasp.

'I'm callin' you, Raybold. You're too crooked to live and that's why you're gonna die!'

'No, Curt!' Don Luis shouted.

'Damn you – this is my play. Draw, or die a coward, Raybold! I swore I'd get you both, big man!'

To keep his hand clear of his Colt was the hardest thing Raybold had ever called upon himself to do. But he managed it, even as August continued raging. Then suddenly the full impact of what the other had said, struck home. '*Both*!'

'Earl!' he breathed. 'You backshot him!'

'Damned right I did! Now you join him, Raybold!'

August's draw was a thing of perfection, a blistering clear that brought up the gun faster than a man could blink.

But if the man was lightning fast then Duane Raybold's draw was driven by a once in a lifetime necessity that saw him complete his fastest ever draw and trigger off that cannon blast of murderous sound which shook the room and left his enemy sprawled upon the floor, never to move again.

'It was him or me, Don Luis,' Duane panted in the massive silence that followed the shooting.

'I know,' sighed the don, haggard and bent. 'Very well, *señor*, there has been too much death. You may tell Ben McQueen I shall meet him at ten tomorrow at the Court House in Fort Such.'

The betting in the saloons of Fort Such was all on failure. There was too much hatred, shed blood and far too much hunger for revenge on both sides – or so the babbling bookmakers contended.

There followed three grim days of tension and saloons brawls and dire predictions of a six-gun holocaust – before Juan Mariano and Libby McQueen lost patience with their elders and defiantly agreed to quit waiting for a more peaceable climate to stage their nuptials. So they went ahead and booked the church for as soon as possible – which happened to be that very afternoon.

Everyone said they were loco. Maybe they were. But a shrewd handful shared the belief that if the union of the town's handsomest and best-liked young couple couldn't bring this lousy town to its senses, nothing could. Ever.

It was, as everybody eventually agreed later, the finest wedding in the town's history. The bride was stunning and the groom wore a six-gun as a caution against any fool who might try to ruin his wedding. Yet somehow the ceremony went off without a hitch while the celebrations which followed lasted all night long without so much as a punch being thrown in anger.

There was rice and confetti and hearty cheers as the handsome couple clambered up into Juan's spring cart and wheeled away, leaving a yawning vacuum of silence behind them as old enemies regarded one another with renewed suspicion. And trouble was surely in the wind before a sudden cheer erupted from the saloon and the crowd in the street swung to see upon a high veranda along the street, two men greeting each other sheepishly and then patting each other on the back.

Moments later Don Luis and Ben McQueen actually got around to shaking hands.

The Pierro County range war was over at last – and not before time.

Cresting a gentle rise that brought the old Raybold spread into full view, they spotted the black horse standing by the hitchrail by the house.

'Well, looks like your hunch was right, Miss Gail,' said driver Mick Clayton. 'That there is Duane's prad right enough, no mistake.'

The girl nodded. 'Drive me down to the trees, please Mick.'

'Anything you say, missy.'

Upon reaching the cottonwoods Clayton halted the rig, lashed the lines about the whip socket then jumped down and helped the girl descend.

Gail was wearing a new outfit from her own store, and as she lifted the hem of her skirt and headed up for the old ranch house, Mick Clayton sighed for his lost youth and wished to heck it were he that Gail was interested in. So he tugged a flask from his hip pocket for consolation.

Passing the hitching rail the girl immediately saw that the black horse was carrying Raybold's packroll. Rounding a corner she hurried on until halted by the sight of Raybold standing upon the gallery.

The gunfighter stood with one shoulder leaning against an upright while staring at the limitless nothingness of the far horizon. He appeared lost in thought until the girl came up from behind and spoke his name.

He whirled. 'Gail! What the heck are you doing out here?'

'I might well ask you the same thing, Duane.'

Raybold appraised her as he descended the

steps. 'You look very . . . very pretty today,' he said formally, almost awkwardly.

'Thank you. I-I thought I might find you here today. I saw your horse. You're leaving, aren't you?'

'That's so. Just came out to say goodbye to the old place.'

'But you weren't going to say goodbye to me, were you?'

'I-I figured you'd understand why I didn't, Gail.'

'I'm afraid I don't. You'll have to explain it to me.'

Raybold was ill at ease, something rare for him. 'Some things are best not talked to death, Gail. It's best I just ride out and we start forgetting about one another.'

'Why is that best? Please, Duane, I need to know.'

'Please, Gail, I—'

'It wouldn't be because you love me, by any chance, would it? That wouldn't be the reason you couldn't simply say goodbye?'

They stood in the sun for a long silent moment before Raybold finally nodded. 'I guess that is the reason if it comes right down to cases, Gail.'

The girl was suddenly smiling even though plainly not far from tears. 'Oh, Duane,' she breathed. Then her voice changed, grew almost stern. 'But why were you quitting this way if—?'

'You'd have to know why,' he cut in. 'After all that's happened . . . after all the hell I raised here, there's nothing for it but for me to go.'

She drew closer, lovelier than he'd ever seen her. 'Nothing so terrible happened that can't be forgotten, Duane. The night the town realized why you'd come back, they were ready to lynch you. But this morning's issue of the *Sentinel* is referring to you as the man who saved Pierro County.'

'Is that true?'

'Yes. Maybe you did some things that were wrong – way back. But nobody in Pierro County is blameless.'

'Do you really believe that?'

She took his hands in hers. 'I surely do. So you see, there's really no reason why you should leave . . . unless you truly want to, that is?'

'I sure don't,' he replied, gazing out over the old spread. 'Y'know, my one big idea on returning from the war was to start ranching again!'

'Then do it, Duane – do it.' Releasing his hands Gail walked a short distance towards the house, then turned to face him. 'Yes, I think we can save the old place.'

'We?'

'My goodness, Duane Raybold, for somebody who did so much talking during the peace negotiations, you can sound awfully tongue-tied. You *are* going to ask me to marry you, aren't you?'

Raybold was stunned. With peace finally settled over Fort Such, he'd quit town early that morning fully aware he was leaving behind perhaps the two people closest to him in life, Earl Parnell and Gail James.

He'd meant merely to stop by the old place to say goodbye to the memories before riding on out – most likely to resume his gunfighting career – and definitely never to return to Pierre County again.

But all that had been changed in a matter of minutes. He'd known for a long time he was desperately and hopelessly in love with Gail James, but had never dreamed she might return his feelings. Yet the way she looked at him now was more convincing than mere words could ever be.

'Gail,' he said softly. 'Will you marry me?'

'Yes, Duane darling, oh *yes*!'

He moved to take her in his arms, then paused. Unbuckling the heavy, hand-tooled Mexican gunrig, he gazed down soberly at the big Colts.

He'd once practised four hours every day with these weapons, seven days a week. They were the tools of his bitter revenge, his lethal companions over the long and dangerous years.

He needed them no longer.

The gunbelt thudded to the ground. Then feeling clean and free in a way he'd not known in seven long years, Duane Raybold took the girl he loved in his arms.